# The Sea is Singing

# The Sea is Singing

## Rosalind Kerven

Blackie

for Richard (again), for everything

British Library Cataloguing in Publication Data
Kerven, Rosalind
The sea is singing.
I. Title     II. Rijnsburger, Ietje
823'.914[J]          PZ7

ISBN 0-216-91838-3




Blackie and Son Limited
Furnival House
7 Leicester Place
London WC2H 7BP

Printed in Great Britain

# Contents

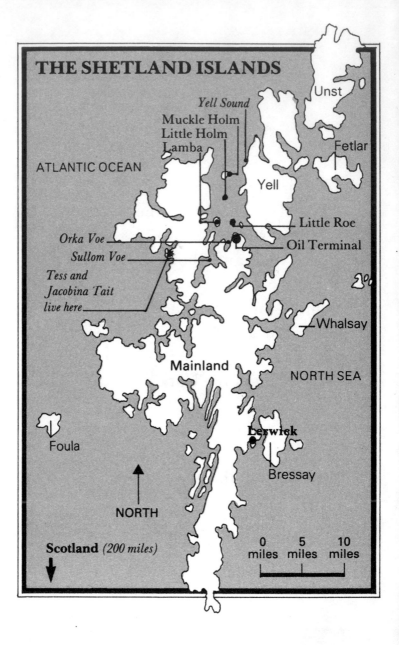

# 1

## The First Singing

Listen.

I wish that you could hear it.

It came to me through a storm: the sea broke and broke, it swept me deep into its secrets. It was scary and beautiful and sad, what I heard, and it changed my life.

But there are some things I ought to explain to you before I start.

When all this happened, I lived right in the north of Scotland, in the Shetland Islands. I like it there: all the colours have a soft, watery rainbow light and the air tastes salty-clean from the ocean. But the wind can roar, and the sea roars, and in winter the darkness goes on and on.

It's a long way from anywhere else.

In the old days, the men netted their lives around the sea, and the women used to knit their fingers into a tangle of wool and lace and Fair Isle patterns. But there's more, much more to tell you later, about the patterns.

When I was still little, they started drilling for oil. They built a weird steel and concrete terminal at the end of Sullom Voe, and soon the night sky behind the hills was set alight by the ghostly glow of oil flares.

My dad's pretty brainy, and he got a really important job to do with the oil. When he went to work, it

7

was as if he drove through the gates of that terminal into an alien, automaton world.

My name's Teresa, by the way: most people call me Tess. I was twelve years old when these things started.

I can remember the date: November 13th. It was almost dark before three o'clock. The wind had been howling up to storm speed all day, and the sea was throwing itself right up. Our house was at the end of a lonely road, just a short way from the cliffs, and when the waves were stirred up like this, the whole place seemed to shudder in its very foundations.

It was Saturday, but my dad was working. Although he was meant to be home by lunch-time, he still hadn't come; and with rain and sleet battering against the windows like fistfuls of gravel, Mum was getting jittery.

"He's had an accident Tess, you see! The car's been blown off the road—or he's stranded out on one of the rigs . . ."

I was only half listening. Clouds glowered down over the cold, thickening twilight, but my sheep-dog Freya was whining: she wanted to go out.

"Take care," Mum fussed at me as I pulled on my oilskins. "Don't you go far in all this weather, Tess—I don't want you gone missing as well. Stick to the path . . ."

I nodded, stepping into my wellingtons.

". . . and whatever you do, keep right away from the cliffs!"

We squeezed out through the back door, Freya and I, and shut it firmly before the storm could blow in. We both shivered; then struck out, fast and urgent, to get warm.

As soon as the twilight had swallowed us out of sight, we left the rough track and turned straight towards the sea. It was mostly coarse, sheep-cropped grass on the cliffs—easy enough to cross, even in bad weather, so long as you watched out for jagged pebbles, slithery ropes of seaweed and broken shells dropped by the birds.

Freya went galloping ahead, her thick black and white fur plastered to a smooth sheen by the rain. I could just see her silhouette, waiting for me on the cliff's edge, barking.

I came to crouch beside her, and we watched the churning sea together for a while.

I was stroking her absent-mindedly, when suddenly, under my fingers, her muscles then her whole body seized. She stood frozen as if to pounce, ears cocked, eyes fixed on the driving curtain of rain.

"What's the matter?" I whispered.

She twitched and a collar of fur on her neck stood ominously up on end.

There was not much light left: no moon or stars penetrated the swirling thicket of cloud, and I couldn't see anything by the distant oil-glow. Behind the cliff, yellow squares of lamplight marked our house, and there was a faint twinkle from old Miss Tait's cottage, a long way off along the road.

But before us, where Freya stared, there was nothing.

I threw off my hood and listened.

I heard the elements. I heard Freya, panting soft and fast beside me.

And I heard singing.

Deep and sonorous, wordless, formless, it floated towards us with the rain and wind off the sea.

I began to sweat inside the oilskins and felt the hair on the back of my own neck rise, like Freya's.

I stood up straight and strained to listen. Sometimes I could hear it quite clearly; then the tempest seemed to swallow it almost away.

Maybe, I thought, it's only my imagination. I was tingling all over, so I told myself quietly, firmly: you're dreaming it, you're dreaming it. Here in the lonely darkness, I thought, it's easy to think things that don't exist.

Then I looked at Freya and knew that I was wrong. She could hear it too.

A great gust blew off the sea, and the storm came on louder. The Singing shot towards us: slow and long it was, then faster, sharper—until at last it broke and fell into eerie, cloistered silence, like a shattering of star-dust.

Freya shook herself out of her trance.

"What was it?" My own words hovered in the mist. It was quiet now, yet the Singing still clung to me, a calling I couldn't shake off.

I turned and stumbled home, still trembling, with Freya cowering and whimpering at my heel.

Back in our bright kitchen, Mum toasted fruit bannocks while I towelled Freya down. Just as tea was ready and the bannocks oozing butter, the door opened and Dad burst in, looking tired and agitated, and shouting that he was starving.

"You might have rung!" cried Mum. "Tess and I were wondering where on earth you were."

"Had a bit of a problem," said Dad with his mouth already full. "Emergency. Couldn't just leave it."

"What's happened?"

11

"Bit of an oil leak. Can't work out where it's coming from."

I wrenched my mind away from the cliff-tops and started to listen.

"Reckon it's the new system," Dad went on. "The conservation people will have a field day if they catch on. They'll be wanting us to stop the whole operation."

"Well you ought to," said Mum, "if it's causing pollution."

"What's the new system?" I asked.

"It's a grand little idea. Bit difficult to explain simply, but it's a sort of revolution in engineering. It could change the whole shape of oil extraction, speed it up, get us all rich. It could make Shetland oil the cheapest in the world."

"But it's not much good if it's leaking," said Mum, "and you have to shut it down."

He chewed hard on his bannock for a few moments, looking grave and distant. "No it's not," he said at last.

"Dad," I said, "Are you worried about it?"

He forced a smile at me. "Worried? Not me, Tess. I've always said, work's important but not worth getting into a sweat about. Any more tea in the pot?"

Mum filled up his cup.

"Now let's see," he went on brightly, "this weekend we were all going to talk about Christmas, weren't we? How many weeks is it . . . ?"

That smile still played about his mouth, but his eyes looked worn out and somehow distant. I went to him, and he flung an arm around my waist; but I could tell his mind was neither on Christmas nor on me.

12

"Thought what you want from us yet, Tess?"

"No, not really." Watching him, I knew he wouldn't have listened properly, even if I had. "Dad, how long will you have off this year?"

"Oh," he said lightly, "that's not decided yet. It's still a long time away. Christmas Day, certainly, probably a day or two more."

"Is that *all*?"

"Maybe more, Tess, it all depends on what happens with . . . on how busy we are."

"On what happens with what? This emergency you just said about?"

"Surely not," said Mum. "It'll be blown over long before then, won't it love? You're always having crises out there, it seems to me; and then two days later you've forgotten all about them."

"That's right," said Dad, still looking distant.

"So you won't let the sea be polluted or anything?" I pressed him.

"Over my dead body, that's for sure!"

The phrase made me shiver as if it were an omen. Mum noticed and—typically—misunderstood.

"You're still cold, Tess," she scolded, and then added for Dad's benefit; "She got soaked through on the cliffs with that wretched dog of hers. Came in after dark looking like she'd seen a ghost."

"Oho," said Dad, "early night for you then, Tess?"

There was a kindness in his voice, but all the same I could tell that really he wanted me away so that he could talk to Mum alone.

"Have a hot bath," coaxed Mum, as if she was part of the conspiracy, "then snuggle up warm with a book or something. We don't want you catching a chill."

13

I didn't stay long in the bath. The roar of water pouring from the taps brought back the storm song again: I didn't want to hear it.

Mum brought me cocoa in bed and I tried to settle down and read, but I couldn't concentrate.

The storm rattled at my window, like someone trying to break in.

I lay down, to doze or think instead.

I couldn't do either.

My mind churned like the waves I'd watched with Freya: all I could see was the disturbing, worn-out coldness in my father's eyes; and when I managed to push that away, my head filled again ... with the Singing.

I began to think that maybe I *had* to keep on remembering it, that it was something uniquely, mysteriously important.

But for the life of me, I couldn't fathom out what, or why.

# 2

## *Learning to Side-step*

There was no-one at home I could ask about it. And the only neighbour we had was Miss Tait, who was so sunken and lined you could scarcely even guess her age. Tall, spindly and stooping she was. She'd lived out on the Ness since before we came, but she'd never tell anyone for how long, or where she'd originally come from.

Mum used to keep a kindly eye on her. On Sunday she said, "Pop across and see Miss Tait this afternoon, there's a dear. She'll be wanting some eggs and the papers."

"Me?" I'd never been to her poky house on my own before.

"I'm so busy, Tess, with Dad not having time to lend a hand. She won't bite you."

So I took Freya for moral support. Miss Tait lived just off the road, down a track that was a mess of thick brown mud and puddles. The sky that morning was white and bright and dry, but still full of wind and spray.

Her cottage was like something that had oozed up out of the moors, a stone-encrusted toadstool. It was rough and uneven, colourless, built low and squashed to resist the gales.

The patch where her garden might have been was a wilderness of untamed grass and weeds, turned dead and papery by the winter. And in the middle of this little jungle stood something that had always puzzled me: an elegantly shaped, barnacle-encrusted wooden boat.

There was no bell and no knocker. I banged with my fist on the peeling blue paint of the front door, but nothing happened.

So I began rattling the latch up and down and Freya set up a barking; and presently we heard footsteps shuffling and the door swung open to a musty gloom.

Jacobina Tait peered down at us, her wrinkles folding into the barest hint of a smile.

"Teresa, isn't it?"

"Mum sent some eggs," I said holding out the basket, "and wanted to see that you're all right."

"Me? I'm all right I suppose," she said crossly. She hesitated, narrowing her hollow eyes at me and rubbing her chin as if pondering something of great importance. "Well, you'd better come in, since you're here, Teresa, come in."

"Can I bring Freya?"

She bent to look doubtfully at the dog.

"Is he clean?"

"*She!*" I corrected her.

"All right, all right then, *is* she? I don't want piddle on my floors."

Behind her I could just see the overcrowded sitting room, a threadbare jumble of dusty knick-knacks and furniture.

"I've trained her," I said indignantly. "She never makes a mess."

"Come on then. But wipe your feet—*and* the dog's! Now I'll put the kettle on. Sit down, Teresa, sit down."

Inside, the stuffiness made me want to gasp. I found a seat in a battered, lop-sided armchair with one leg shorter than the others, and Freya settled obediently at my feet. Miss Tait set a big black kettle on her old-fashioned kitchen range, and sat down stiffly opposite me.

"It'll take a while to boil," she said. "The peat's burning badly today. The wind's wrong. You're not in a hurry, I hope?"

I swallowed. "Oh no."

We sat in silence for a few moments. I couldn't think what on earth to say.

"Now then, Teresa, it's Sunday isn't it? Well, what are you doing with yourself?"

"Oh, walking," I said. "Looking at things. I like watching the sea."

"Yes," she said, "so do I." She was staring directly at me. "What other things do you like looking at Teresa?"

I thought. "Well. Anything really."

"Do you like *old* things? Antiques?"

I glanced nervously at the assortment of faded china junk that was crammed along her shelves.

"Sort of."

"When I was a girl," said Miss Tait, "I used to *love* old things. My father brought me gifts back from the Indies, from the Seven Seas. Wonderful carved and painted things they were. I used to think they were magic." She leaned suddenly towards me. "Do *you* believe in magic, Teresa?"

She spoke with such earnestness, that I could tell the question was meant seriously.

I considered for a moment.

17

"I think I used to, when I was younger. But no, not now."

She nodded.

"But I wonder—do you have a strong imagination? You're still young enough . . . when I was your age, when I used to look at the sea . . . Teresa, *doesn't it ever set you dreaming?*"

I felt that she knew I had a secret, though I couldn't think how she did. I felt she was going to worm it out of me, inch by inch.

I said, "My teachers always tell me day-dreaming's bad."

"Then they're ignorant so-and-so's!" said Miss Tait firmly. "It's day-dreaming that makes inventors, and poets and philosophers. What kind of a moron are they trying to turn you into at that school of yours? If you haven't got an imagination yet girl, I'd better show you how. Look at this."

She got up and, taking a small box from one of her shelves, put it into my hands. It was black, and so lacquered that it reflected light almost like a mirror. There were peculiar figures painted all over it: blue men with eight arms like a spider, bright pink veiled maidens riding horses with thick curling manes, elongated lions, leopards and unicorns. It was a sort of tiny, doll-sized cabinet, with lots of drawers, cupboards and panels.

"What is it?"

"One plays with it," said Miss Tait, rubbing her long bony fingers up and down. "One opens it up—and thinks. See what's inside. It comes from the East. I used to call it my Dreaming Box."

I pulled open the drawers. There was a tiny treasure carefully laid in each: a pressed violet, fine as tissue paper, a flake of orange coral, an ear of barley, a scatter of coloured grains of sand.

"It's beautiful," I said.

"You haven't seen it all yet. What about the bottom panel?"

I felt it all over.

"How does it open?"

"Use your brain, Teresa, use your imagination."

There was no handle or catch to it that I could see, no means of pulling it out. I began to feel sweaty and dry-tongued, like when a teacher picks on you for a question that there's not a chance you can answer.

"I can't open it. I don't know how to."

"*I'm* not going to tell you. You *must* work it out for yourself." She sounded unexpectedly severe. "Side-step in your mind, think, Teresa, *think*."

I closed my eyes and thought hard. From the very edge of my mind's eye, something seemed to nudge me: I made a great effort to focus on it. It came: I dragged it and the idea came. And then it was easy. I opened my eyes again and turned the box over. I pressed my finger-tips on the back. The panel sprung open at once.

"Good! I knew you could! Well done!"

Inside, there was another little box. And inside that, another. And so they went on, getting smaller and smaller like a set of those wooden Russian dolls, until in the very last one I found a tiny golden key.

"The key," said Miss Tait, "to everything."

"I don't understand."

"It's not a toy," she said, "but a lesson. You'll understand it by and by."

She put her shrivelled face very close to mine.

"There'll be mysteries," she said. "You might have

19

to puzzle them out. Just remember this box and what it has taught you. Make your mind side-step, if you can't find the answer: it's usually very simple. Look inside and inside, and in the end you will find the key."

That's when I knew I ought to ask her about the noises. But I couldn't think how to begin.

"Miss Tait," I whispered, "how did you get so wise?"

She smiled—properly this time—and shook her head.

"The kettle's boiling."

She busied herself with pot and caddy, measuring the tea out with a large spoon. I noticed that on her wedding finger she wore a gold ring with a blue sapphire. Where had she come from, what had she done with her life?

"Sugar? Milk?"

The tea looked thick and unappetising. I balanced it on a rickety side-table and hoped she wouldn't notice if I didn't drink it.

But she sat there staring at me.

"I think, Teresa, that there's something you rather want to ask me."

I opened my mouth.

"We were talking," she prompted me, "a while back, about day-dreaming while you look at the sea."

"Oh . . ."

"Now then?"

"Miss Tait," I whispered, "have you ever heard . . . I mean . . . can the sea *sing*?"

In the long silence, I heard the peats shifting softly inside the stove. Gradually the old lady's eyes drew my gaze upwards like a magnet, until we met each other, deep and direct.

"Ah," she said slowly, "so you *are* the one."

"What do you mean?"

Freya sat up suddenly and began to watch Miss Tait, alert and keen.

"You can be trusted," she said, "with an errand."

"I don't understand."

"No, but you will, by and by. Messages . . ."

"Messages?"

". . . from the sea. Listen, Teresa, when it comes, you mustn't fight it. There'll be a reason . . . Ah, your father! He's with the oil. What's he been doing?"

"Doing?"

"What's new? Why should there be messages? There must be something serious . . ."

I remembered that conversation over bannocks about the oil leak, and my insides went all cold.

"I don't know," I said quickly.

"No matter, no matter, it will come. Now, this errand. You'll be at school in Lerwick tomorrow?"

I nodded.

"Will you deliver something for me?"

"All right." Freya was still watching her, fascinated. "But what is it?"

"It has to go to the knitwear shop, MacBrides. Just a small parcel. But Teresa, listen . . ."

"Yes?"

"It must go only into the right person's hands. Mrs MacBride herself. Do you know her?"

"No."

"Then ask for her. Don't give it to anyone else. Tell her it's from Jacobina. Some . . . *patterns*. She'll understand."

21

I stood up, seeking an escape before she could pin me down with anything else.

"I'd best go. Shall I take the parcel now?"

She shuffled to a door that led off into a back room, then hesitated, her fingers hovering over the handle, as if she didn't want to open it while I was there.

"Ah—no. Later. It's not quite ready. I'll bring it round to you later. Thank you for coming, Teresa." She began to shoo me out. "Thank your mother for the eggs. And the dog—you can bring him again."

"*Her!*"

"She's clean anyway."

"She heard the singing too," I said.

"Did she now? Aha. Well, and you haven't mentioned it to anyone else?"

"No."

"Be careful. There are those who might misinterpret it—or use it the wrong way. An oath of secrecy never did anyone any harm. And Teresa—I'm very sorry about your father."

My heart skipped a great, thudding beat.

"My father? But he's all right! What do you mean?"

"It'll show, soon enough, in the patterns. Perhaps we can save him, after all. I wouldn't like to think . . . after all, he's a kind enough man. I shall tell them that: your family's never seemed to mean any harm. But don't worry yourself, it'll probably come right in the end. These things usually do. Just remember what I've taught you today. Remember to side-step. Remember to look inside and inside, until you come at last to the key."

She went abruptly back in and shut the door.

Freya and I ran all the way home.

22

"There's been a phone-call for you," said Mum when we got there, "from Annie."

Annie Sinclair was my friend from school. She was more or less my *best* friend, actually, if I disregarded the fact that she'd gone all scatty and boring over computers. But I still kept in with her because her brothers, Oliver and Rob, were good fun and I looked up a bit to her older sister Jane. Also I liked visiting them in their big house in the middle of Lerwick.

I rang her back, and she asked me to stay with them after school, over next weekend.

I was glad. For the first time ever, I wanted to get away from home. I was frightened of hearing the Singing again.

Mum was glad too.

"You've been really mopey since last night, Tess. You need some company. It's not good for someone of your age to spend so much time on your own. There's nothing worrying you is there?"

If only she knew!

"No."

I was frightened of seeing Jacobina Tait again, too.

But she came, as promised, at half-past four, carrying a torch to light her way through the winter's evening, with a parcel under her arm.

I pretended to be busy upstairs while Mum answered the door.

"For Teresa," I heard. "She promised she'd run me this errand. It's rather urgent—but I know I can trust her."

"Won't you come in for a moment, Miss Tait?" (She'd never once stepped inside our house.)

"No, I won't, thank you. I'm so busy. Goodbye."

"Well!" laughed Mum, coming back in with the

thing. "Well, well! MacBride's Knitwear Shop, eh? I never knew the old girl went in for knitting! She must sit in that back room that she always keeps locked to do it, because *I've* never seen her! We'll give it to the postman, shall we Tess? You don't want to go traipsing round Lerwick with the wretched thing do you?"

"I don't mind," I said. "I promised."

"Oh, if you've made her a promise you'll have to keep it." She looked curiously at the parcel. "Jacobina Tait's own hand-knits, eh. I wonder what on earth they're like?"

"Does she keep her knitting a secret then? Whatever for?"

"I expect," said Mum, "she's trying to earn a bit on the side to supplement her pension and she doesn't want anyone to know. I mean, look at the crumbling old pig sty she lives in! If the truth were known, she must be desperate for some more money—desperate for something!"

Yes, there had been something almost desperate in the way Jacobina Tait had pinned me down that morning.

# 3

## *"Tell her, They've Come"*

On Monday I slipped out of school as soon as lunch-time started and hurried into town with the parcel.

MacBride's was a small, old-fashioned family business tucked into a sloping alley between Commercial Street and the harbour. I pushed open the door and went in: at once a thick-crisp scent of new wool almost overpowered me. Underfoot, the carpet was wool, muffling footsteps. And the shelves were crammed with wool—sweaters, scarves and skeins for knitting: they too gathered sounds to themselves, turning talk and the ring of the till into a queer, muted hush.

I stood quietly at the end of a queue of customers. At the counter, purchases were wrapped with neat perfection, money and gossip changed hands: there was all the time in the world.

Immediately in front of me, another girl in school clothes was waiting. She was taller, older than me, with straight blond hair hanging almost to her waist. I heard her sigh with impatience at the slowness of it all; then she turned round and flashed me a grin of recognition.

"Tess, hello, what are *you* doing here?"

It was Jane Sinclair, my friend Annie's older sister. But my heart sank. She was in the sixth form and could get me into trouble, if she wanted to, for being out of school.

"Oh, hello. Nothing."

25

She glanced at me curiously.

"Just running an errand."

"I see. You've got permission of course?"

I looked at my shoes.

"I'll wait for you," said Jane. "You won't be long, will you?"

Her turn came: she wanted a pullover for her grandad's birthday or something.

"OK Tess, it's all yours."

I prayed for her to change her mind and leave me: she didn't. We were the only people left in the shop. The assistant, small and mousey, hovered behind the counter.

"Are you Mrs MacBride?" I asked.

"No. Mrs MacBride's at lunch."

"Please could I see her?"

"I'm sorry, she doesn't like to be disturbed. Can't I help you?"

"Come on," hissed Jane, "you can just as well give whatever it is to this lady."

"I've got . . . something for her," I said. The assistant saw the parcel clutched tightly under my arm.

"Oh, no problem, I'll pass it on."

"I was told I must only give it to *her*. To Mrs MacBride herself. Please. Please could you go and tell her—it's . . . *patterns*. From Jacobina."

"Jacobina?" For a split second the assistant's smile faded. "From Jacobina." She licked her lips. "Just a minute then."

She disappeared into a back passage.

"*What* is it?" asked Jane.

On the wall hung a round clock like you see in

pictures of old-fashioned school rooms: its minute hand crept steadily, noisily on.

"Nothing," I said again.

The passage door opened and a middle-aged woman came in. She was plump and rosy cheeked, with a thick head of floppy, gull-grey curls. She must have leaped from her lunch in an awful hurry because she was still chewing as she waddled through, breathing rather heavily and dabbing her mouth with a white cotton handkerchief.

She blinked at us anxiously.

"Someone asking . . . ?"

"Me," I said. "I've got this for you, Mrs MacBride. From Jacobina."

Despite her large frame, she was round the counter in a jiffy, snatching the parcel from me as if afraid it might disappear into thin air.

She felt it carefully, but didn't open it.

"What do you know about Jacobina?"

There was something loaded in that question, a heaviness that belied her motherly appearance. I found courage, for a second, to look her straight in the eye—and met only a thick, impenetrable gaze.

My senses keyed up.

"Miss Tait trusts me," I said carefully. "She said so."

Mrs MacBride jerked a thumb in Jane's direction. "Aye. And what about *her*?"

I could see Jane bridling under the insult.

"She's . . . we're at school together," I said.

"Well," said Mrs MacBride, "remember to keep your mouth shut, that's all. The less that know the better."

Jane grabbed my arm and began to march me out

of the shop. "Come along, Tess, we must go. Excuse us Mrs MacBride, we have to be back by two."

In the street outside, I confronted her.

"Jane, that was rude!"

"Well she was rude to me. Pointing like that, talking as if I wasn't there!"

"But I hadn't finished yet. She was in the middle of saying something. She might have had an important message for me to take back."

"Tess, what on *earth* are you gabbling on about? You're the one who'll be in trouble with the Head if we're late."

She hurried me through the drizzle, stumbling over uneven paving stones, dodging cars and people. The shop-fronts seemed to glower over us in the winding street. I longed to go back, to hear the things still left unsaid . . .

We'd reached a quiet terrace of old grey cottages standing sheer against the water-front, when footsteps came clomping up behind us and a voice called, "Just wait, I've something for you!"

It was Mrs MacBride again, red and puffing, a plastic rain-cape draped hastily round her ample shoulders.

"Thank goodness I caught you. I don't want to make you girls late but—I'm sorry, what was your name?"

I told her.

"Tess, would you mind taking this to her?"

"To Miss Tait?"

"Yes. I think she'll be expecting it."

"What is it?" Jane drew herself up, fingering her prefect's badge with carefully manicured nails. "It's not right, Mrs MacBride, for young Tess here to have to keep running errands when she's supposed to be at school."

"I don't mind," I said quickly.

Mrs MacBride shot Jane a long, penetrating look. Muddy, her expression was, dark and obscure like a moorland pool.

"It's wool," she said, "that's all."

I took the parcel.

Even just holding it in my hand, I knew it wasn't wool. It was too heavy.

I decided to test her. "Is it more *patterns*?" I asked.

"Aye," said Mrs MacBride. For the breath of a moment, the muddiness drew back and she smiled at me—a welcoming smile, so it seemed. "Patterns it is. I think Jacobina's been expecting them for some time. So you can tell her, Tess—*they've come*."

She seemed to be making a great effort to sound ordinary and lighthearted, but it didn't quite work.

"You can tell her, now it's starting, we'll be needing her services quite a lot." She glanced aside at Jane. "Her knitting services, of course."

"Right," said Jane firmly, tapping her watch. "Now Tess, come *on*—we'll have to run."

She dragged me off, leaving Mrs MacBride staring after us.

"Keep up with me!" I could tell she was searching for some way to enforce her will. "I'll get you a detention if you go crawling back to that silly woman again!"

We jogged side by side in silence for a while. The school was just in sight when she doubled up.

"It's no good, I've got a stitch . . . *wait* for me Tess!"

"You wouldn't wait for me when I was . . ."

30

"That doesn't matter, you should have respect for your elders," she panted, clutching her side. "And listen, what's going on with that Mrs MacBride?"

I tried to make light of it.

"I don't know. I was running an errand for a neighbour, that's all."

She tossed her long yellow hair, back to the left, back to the right, behind her shoulders. "Then why were you both saying things as if you didn't want me to hear? What have you got there? And what did *you* give to her?"

"I haven't a clue. Boring old knitting wool, I suppose."

"Fibber! *Tell* me, Tess!"

She made to grab me: I skipped out of her way, trying to dash the last few yards through the school gates before she could catch me up. But she could run faster than me.

"Jane—" I tried to play for time. "Annie's asked me to stay at your house on Saturday. I'll try to . . . try to find out by then and tell you what the parcels are. Honestly."

"Hmmm . . . OK then Tess." There was teasing in her voice. "I'd better mention to Annie and Oliver and Rob that you've promised to reveal something really exciting when you come!"

I thought of warnings, of two different urgent hints at the need for secrecy. "I'm sure there's nothing exciting about it at all," I said lamely.

She smiled sweetly, and tapped my parcel as if it contained some delicious surprise for *her*.

"But all the same, Tess, I'm itching to know. You won't forget, will you?"

# 4

# Oaths in Blood

Annie pushed open the front door and clattered down the long, hollow hallway to the stairs. Her voice echoed carelessly between the high walls.

"Jane says you've got a secret to tell us all, Tess. Any chance of a preview?"

"No," I said firmly. I dumped my weekend bag down.

"Come straight up. You might as well leave all your stuff in our room."

Annie shared the large, sloping attic with Jane. It was three flights of stairs to the top of their house.

On the ground floor, Mr and Mrs Sinclair had their surgeries: they were both doctors. When you went in, everything smelt of polish and disinfectant: sometimes you bumped into patients who wished you good day in polite, worried tones.

Upstairs and upstairs there were endless doors, it seemed, to living rooms, best rooms and bedrooms. I'd never seen inside them all: whenever I was there, we spent most of our time in the attic.

Annie was in there already when I caught her up, straightening her bed, cramming things in drawers. We both changed into jeans, and fetched milk and biscuits from the kitchen.

"Let's get our homework done first."

She helped me with my maths and I gave her some ideas for English: that's the way it was between us.

Then she switched on her micro-computer—pride and joy of her last birthday—and we spent a happy hour playing some new space-games on it.

"*Bor-ing!*"

The door opened and Rob burst in. He was eleven, small for his age, but sharp and confident.

"Turn that stupid machine off! We want to talk to Tess."

"To me?" I said, flattered.

"Who else?" Oliver came in behind his brother and flopped lankily to the floor. He was a year or two older than us. He had an odd way of blinking from behind his glasses, but I liked him well enough: he never once laughed at any of the things I said.

The computer flickered and bleeped. Annie still sat glued to it, twiddling knobs, pulling absent-mindedly on strands of her straggly brown hair.

"I can't hear myself think!" complained Rob. He pulled the plug out. "Useless object! Makes electrical interference on the brain, that's what I reckon . . ."

"Rubbish!" Annie leaped at him, furious. "Just you wait—"

"Stop rowing," interjected Oliver. "Hands up who wants to know what Tess was up to in the wool shop last week?"

They were of one mind on that, at any rate. I began to feel nervous.

"We'd better wait for Jane," said Annie.

"Where is she anyway?" asked Rob.

"Little boys who can't guess shouldn't be told. She'll be back soon."

As soon as she came, I was again the centre of attention. Jane said, "Right then, Tess, don't forget

33

your promise to reveal all. Tell us the truth about Mrs MacBride."

I tried to wriggle out of it, but that only made things worse. "I . . . I can't tell you now, not yet."

"Why ever not? You've got to."

"It'll have to wait until later." I floundered desperately. "Till midnight."

"Sounds more intriguing than ever," said Oliver, "but why?"

"Um . . . walls might have ears," I said, "in the day time."

"Don't be daft," said Jane. "No-one will hear us up here. *I* can't stay awake all night: I need my beauty sleep."

"And we all know why!" chorused the others.

Jane flushed scarlet. She got up with a curious jerky movement and stormed to the door. "I'm going to wash my hair. And as for you two—" she turned to the boys "—when I get back, you'd better *scram!*"

"What's up with her?" I asked.

"The lady's in love," said Oliver, "that's all."

I hoped maybe they'd all fall asleep early and forget the whole business, but the Sinclairs have memories like elephants.

I'd just settled comfortably in my sleeping-bag at the end of Annie's bed, when someone tapped on the door. It creaked open and a torch dotted light about the room.

"Just gone midnight," came Rob's voice. "Wake up everyone."

Annie slid out of bed at once. I pretended to snore, but it was no use: they shone the torch directly on me. I gave in just in time to stop Rob squeezing a wet rag over my face.

Jane sighed from across the room: "This is ridiculous! I'm almost asleep. Can't you tell us the secret tomorrow?"

"It's now or never," I said thickly.

"I'll have to listen from my bed then."

She turned over and lay very still. Afterwards, I was never quite sure: had she heard everything we said, or not?

"Have a chocolate," said Oliver, passing round a box. "Now young Teresa, begin!"

And so I began. I told them all about old Miss Tait and how she'd sent Mrs MacBride a mysterious parcel, and about the one Mrs MacBride had sent her back. I'd left it the same evening on Miss Tait's doorstep, then scooted away before she could find it—so I honestly had no idea what either of them contained.

"Is that *all*?" asked Rob when I'd finished.

I nodded; but they couldn't see me in the dark.

"Of course it isn't," said Oliver. "She hasn't explained anything."

The night was a cold, black shroud. I pulled the sleeping-bag up round my shoulders. Half of me longed to share all the spookiness with them. And yet . . .

"If they find out . . ." I faltered.

"*What?*" cried Rob.

"Sshh!"

"We keep secrets to ourselves," urged Annie. "Always. Honestly."

"Swear it!" I said. "Swear an oath then, all of you!"

I was more scared than you might realise. Supposing Miss Tait was a sort of witch? What would she do if she knew I'd broken faith?

35

"May we drop down dead if we give anything away," said Rob quickly. "Is that good enough?"

"I don't know . . ."

"A *written* oath might be better," said Annie.

"Written in *blood*," said Oliver. "Just to make sure. Who's got a pin?"

Annie fetched one, and a notebook, stumbling in the torchlit dark.

"You'd better put something first," Oliver said to me, "to cover yourself."

So I took a pin and pricked my thumb until the blood spurted, thick and red. I was too worked up to notice if it hurt.

"What shall I say?"

"You ought to make it olde Englishe," suggested Annie, "to sound more important."

I dipped the pin in my blood while Rob held the torch steady over the page. Something must have inspired me, because I managed to scrawl:

> *I, Teresa Jamieson, swear by the Singing that I tell secrets to my good friends the Sinclairs on the understanding that their lips are ever sealed.*

"Excellent," said Oliver. "But what do you mean, 'swear by the Singing', Tess?"

I'd written the words despite myself: they'd appeared without being willed.

They all waited.

"I . . . it's part of the secret. Now, you've all got to do it."

They pricked themselves one by one and wrote,

> *Cross my heart and hope to die*
> *if this pledge of secrecy proves a lie,*

each with a signature underneath.

Across the room, Jane was breathing, soft and steady. So much, I thought, for *her* curiosity.

"Now then," said Oliver, "you can't put it off any longer."

So this time I told them all the things that Miss Tait and Mrs MacBride had said. None of them could make sense of it.

"The question is," said Annie, "why did this Miss Tait give her parcel to you in the first place? Why didn't she just post it? I know you're her neighbour and all that—but I mean—you don't know her that well, do you?"

"Not really. No, hardly at all."

"Then how did she know she could trust you?"

My mouth felt dry.

"I think . . . I'm not sure."

Oliver shone the torch right into my face.

"Tess, you *still* haven't told us everything have you? Even though we've sworn in blood. Why?"

"You mustn't laugh then," I cried. "You'll think I'm mad."

"We'll decide that when we've heard all of what you've got to say," said Rob. "Come on then, Miss Jamieson."

"Turn the torch off," said Annie. "You're wasting the battery."

I felt braver in the unbroken dark.

"I think she trusts me because she knows I heard the Singing."

"*That*," whispered Oliver, "what you wrote. What was it?"

I tried to tell them, the eeriness of what I'd heard. Though it was a week gone past, still the memory

37

hung stark and clear in my mind. Yet it was hard to find words to describe it.

To my relief, they all took it seriously.

"You . . . you don't think I'm round the bend?"

"No," said Oliver solemnly, "not me."

The others agreed. I wanted to cry with relief.

"There must be a sensible explanation," said Annie.

We went through all the obvious things, like fog-horns, aircraft noises or submarines, but none of them fitted.

"It seemed to come straight off the sea. It didn't sound like people or machines."

"If you were to hear it again," said Oliver, "do you think you could manage to get it on a tape-recorder?"

"I haven't got one."

"Borrow ours. We've got a small portable one. We'll show you how to use it."

"If you get it," said Rob excitedly, "we could send it to the British Museum or somewhere, for analysis."

"It's *secret*," I hissed at him. "Remember your oath. Written in blood."

Rob swallowed. "Oh. Yup. Heck."

"Listen," said Annie. "If you can get these noises recorded, Tess, I could try and feed them through the computer."

"What good will that do?"

"None at all," said Rob. "It's just another excuse for her silly little games."

"I can't be bothered to thump you," said Annie. "It's a waste of my creative energy. And I need every ounce of it. I'm going to try and write a program based on this Singing. The chances are, it's all got a completely logical meaning."

38

I said, "I wish it *did* have."

"Oh it has," said Annie, "I'm sure *everything* has. The whole universe is logical once you understand it."

"You're wrong, kid," said Oliver slowly. "Logic's just a starting point. I reckon there could be things beyond our wildest dreams lurking right behind it."

# 5

# Long Notes and Short Ones

They showed me carefully how to use the tape recorder and I practised with it a few times to make sure that I could work it. The next weekend I spent at home; and as soon as I could on Saturday morning I went out on the cliffs to try it.

It was an unusually warm, still day for November. There was a fine mist in the air, dampening earth, sand and stones, veiling the distant islands out to sea with the mystery of shadows.

Freya ran happily around, pawing at seaweed, snuffling out rabbit holes, while I played at taping her barks and the sloshing of the waves, lots of innocent things like that.

I really liked it out there with no-one in sight, just sea and sky, grass and rocks. I wasn't scared of the loneliness.

That is, until the Singing started again.

Soft and vague it came at first, insubstantial as the sea-mist hanging. Then it grew louder, more defined.

The Singing was growing closer. It was coming in to me.

I stood motionless, straining, listening. I could feel my heart going thump-thump-thump. I scarcely dared to breathe.

All at once I remembered the tape recorder. My fingers were clumsy with panic, but I managed to set the microphone and turn all the switches on. I was so careful to follow the instructions exactly right, that I even repeated them out loud to be sure that nothing had been forgotten.

I crouched there on my heels, waiting while the Singing rose and fell with the waves and the tape went slowly round.

Then it stopped.

I stopped the tape too, wound it back and pressed the button that said 'play'.

No sound came out.

I cursed and stopped the tape. But I'd done absolutely everything right, I had, I had!

I wound it back and played the tape again, turning the volume up as far as it would go. This time I caught some faint sea-noises, and the shrieking of a lone gull that had passed overhead. Good, I thought, the Singing will come on in a minute..

It didn't.

I wanted to cry.

I looked around for Freya, and whistled for her. She came to me cowering, whining, tail between her legs. She put a muddy paw on my coat, grabbed the hem in her mouth and gently tried to pull me in the direction of home.

"Wait with me Freya," I begged. She crouched obediently at my feet, watching my face with big, anxious eyes.

I grew aware that the Singing had started again. And Freya heard it too, I know she did.

I fiddled with the tape and shouted out loud, "Work, you silly thing, *work*!"

As I picked it up to shake it in my fury, the corner of my eye caught a stretch of grey-green water laid below like a mirror, in the little bay between the cliffs.

Within its depths there was a sudden movement—
something long and dark, sharp enough to make me
jump. It held my eyes, rippling, a ghost of human
form; shaking beyond control, I let the machine drop
from my hands.

It bounced lightly on the springy turf. I heard
footsteps behind and whirled round: the dark, watery
reflection melted out of sight and Miss Tait's voice
said crisply: "Ah, Teresa."

I stammered at her like an idiot: "Oh—oh—oh—
oh"

And the Singing was louder than ever.

She said, "Have you come here to listen?"

"Yes," I whispered. Courage returned, but bringing
with it a disturbing thought: "Can *you* hear it, Miss
Tait—now?"

She laughed and didn't answer.

"What's that contraption you've got there? Are you
trying to make a record of it?"

"It won't work," I said bitterly. "It won't come
out."

It seemed wrong to be talking, all normal, with the
Singing going on and on. As bad as talking through
assembly, or church! Only this kept drawing back
your attention: it was like bassoons and harps, the
sort of music that makes your very insides want to
cry.

"No," said Miss Tait, "I don't suppose it will."

"But *why*?"

"Look at it this way," she said, "it's like waves
coming up a beach. You can see them breaking,
lapping up and up a few more inches, always a bit
further; but if it's the wrong season, they won't reach

42

right up to the highest line of seaweed, not as far as the mark of the highest tide."

She stood there, tall and sunken, as still as I was, leaning on a grey, twisted stick of driftwood and went on: "The Singing's like that, Teresa. It's the wrong season for it to come very far up the shore. It's there all right, coming in, but you have to be close and open to hear it."

"But why can *I* hear it?" I whispered. "Miss Tait, why *me*?"

"I don't know," she said, "but it will come."

"But ought I to—*do* anything about it?"

"It's a warning," she said. "You can't just ignore it, you know."

She turned on her heel and began to shuffle away.

"But Miss Tait—I don't understand!" I cried. "I can't even . . ."

"For goodness sake Teresa!" She paused, not looking at me, but shaking her puckered chin at a distant boulder. "Haven't you learned yet how to think, eh? I taught you to side-step in your mind, didn't I? Think, *think*! Thought is the key, my girl . . ."

She fixed on me suddenly.

"I'll help you then. There are long notes and short ones, aren't there? One can write them down. It's a sort of code." She smiled secretly. "Like braille for blind people. You're blind so far as the Singing goes, I can see that. Now—is that any help to you?"

I could see that she was trying to be kind.

"Yes, thank you," I said weakly.

She nodded, and went on her way.

Back alone, with Freya trembling, and the noises, I was more frustrated now than scared.

I fumbled in my coat pockets: amongst a jumble of

44

string and crab-shells I found what I wanted: a dog-eared notebook and the stub of a pencil.

I stood there listening, sucking the pencil. There were long and short notes, as she'd pointed out. Codes. I closed my eyes and forced myself to concentrate. At last, new thoughts arose from the margins of my mind; in the stillness, it jumped obligingly to one side.

Long and short, codes. Morse Code! I could write it down like that, as dots and dashes. Maybe it was even Morse Code in disguise!

I opened my eyes and listened carefully, then tried to transcribe into symbols what I could hear. Once I got the hang of it, it seemed quite easy: the noises came so slow that I had plenty of time to get them down.

And when I looked at what I'd written, the dots and dashes looked like more than chance: they did seem to fit into a proper sort of pattern . . .

The Singing stopped again. Intuition told me that this time, it was for good. Freya sat up and suddenly seemed brighter; and then the white mist began to lift and a shaft of sunlight came filtering through.

Both times I'd heard the noises, you see, vision had been obscured: the first time by twilight and gales; and now this time by mist.

I remembered a phrase I'd once heard, 'through a glass darkly'. That's how the Singing was to me.

I wondered whether I'd ever hear it on a clear, sunny day.

Still, I had it written down. The whole business was so uncanny that I half expected the notation to fade away before my eyes like forbidden script from some lost, mystic world; it didn't though, of course.

I picked up the tape recorder, called Freya, stuffed the notebook in my pocket and ran home.

When I got there, my dad was talking on the telephone.

Or rather—he wasn't talking but listening. Every now and then he'd utter one or two words in a strange, expressionless way like "Oh lord", and "no no", and "whatever you do, don't touch *that*"; and then there'd be long silences when you could hear another man's voice yabbering down the earpiece and my dad just sat staring at his slippers and shaking his head.

"What's going on?" I asked Mum.

"Work, as usual. An emergency I think."

Dad slammed down the phone.

"I've got to go. At once!"

"Have lunch first," Mum begged him.

"I can't. Sorry love, it won't wait."

He clomped upstairs, reappearing a few minutes later in his office clothes, carrying an overnight bag.

"Don't know when I'll be back—I'll give you a ring, promise. Oh, this blasted pump . . . !"

"The new system?"

Dad nodded. He opened his mouth to say more, then noticing I was there, quickly closed it again.

"What's it about?" I asked.

"Nothing for you to worry about, Tess."

He hurried out, the car started up and he was gone.

Over lunch I prodded Mum about it, but she wasn't telling either.

Afterwards I said, "I'm going to do my homework. Is it all right if I get some books from Dad's study?"

Mum was busy making Christmas cake and things,

46

and she nodded absent-mindedly. I went into the study and shut the door.

I knew the book I wanted: it was a big, dusty volume full of small print and boring diagrams called *Rudiments of Seamanship*. My grandad used to sit and read it like a Bible every afternoon till he got so unwell, he had to go to hospital. When I was little, he used to sit me on his knee and show me pictures in it of old fashioned sailors like he once was, and boats. In the back was a whole chapter about signalling, by flares and semaphore and Morse Code.

I climbed on a chair and pulled the book off the top shelf, then sat myself down at Dad's desk to read. It was heavy and smelt strongly of the half-forgotten tang of Grandad's pipe smoke. The pages were soft and yellow with age.

I found the section on Morse. There was a chart, explaining what all the dots and dashes meant. I pored over it, my eyes flicking from that to the scrap of paper with the Singing written on it, back and forth and back again, until my head began to ache.

But the pattern of dots and dashes before me didn't fit into the chart at all.

"This is hopeless!" I hissed at my notes, through clenched teeth. I felt so fed up that I wanted to screw the lot up and chuck it all in the bin. I wanted to run away from it, from the noises and mysterious messages and Dad working late on Saturdays . . .

My hand began to circle the notebook round and round in a mounting, seething anger.

It upset Dad's papers that were neatly lying underneath. I thought I'd better put them back in place if I could, and as I did so, one of them caught my eye.

Most times, his work's written in a sort of technical

gobbledygook that no-one else could even hope to understand.

But this one was different. The gist of it was quite clear. It said at the top:

*To all staff—emergency alert*

in big red letters. I read on:

*Large oil slick . . . expected to drift out from Sullom Voe . . .*

A disaster! My dad was involved in a major pollution disaster!

*. . . breakdown of the new system . . .*

But the new system was *his*! He'd virtually masterminded it. I skimmed lines and lines of complicated waffle to the bottom:

*Staff are reminded of the high security risk of this venture and that the absolute news blackout on all developments remains until further notice.*

I knew what it all meant. Dad's new system was top secret. This big disaster that was slowly gathering momentum was top secret too, until they could stop it—or until it hit the news with a dreadful, unthinkable bang—

And an awful certainty began to grow in me that the Singing was connected with this in some way.

# 6

# *Ranulf*

"Did you hear it again?" asked Annie. *quickly*

We were changing for gym: I looked conspiratorily around. The other girls were all yacking away at the other end of the changing room; even so, we spoke in whispers.

"Oh yes—I heard it."

"Did you bring the tape recorder back?"

"Yes but—"

"And you managed to record it?"

"No."

Her face fell.

"Annie," I said.

"We *showed* you, Tess, for goodness sake, we thought you'd cottoned on how to do it."

"Annie, you won't believe this, but it didn't come out."

She snorted: "You're just *thick*. Honestly!"

Queueing up for the trampoline, I hissed at her: "It's the wrong frequency."

"What?"

"The Singing. It won't go on the tape. It sort of can't pick it up."

She thought for a moment, then nodded. "I see. Yes, I suppose it makes sense."

Later, we sat together in History. When Mr Fletcher's back was turned to draw something on the blackboard, I slipped her my precious piece of paper.

49

"Guard this with your life."

She peered at it under the desk. "What on earth . . ?"

"The Singing—I wrote it down."

Her eyes began to gleam. "Tess, you're a genius after all!"

In front of us, curious heads turned. We both stared steadfastly, innocently ahead.

"I'll try it on the computer," Annie murmured.

For the rest of that week, I waited impatiently for the result. But each morning she told me she couldn't make anything of it. She thought it might be in another language and was trying to get hold of some foreign programs: perhaps if there was some way of combining Russian, for example, with Morse, we might get somewhere.

It began to seem less and less likely that we'd ever crack it.

By Friday we'd even stopped talking about it.

But over the weekend, I couldn't stop brooding.

"Whatever's the matter?" asked Mum. "Look, I'm going into town this afternoon—why don't you come? Perhaps it'll get you out of your mood."

We did some Christmas shopping together, and then she had an appointment at the hairdresser. We arranged that I'd go over to see the Sinclairs, and Mum would pick me up when she'd finished.

It was already dark when I rang at their door: almost at once, it was flung wide open by Jane. A radiant smile lit her face—but it quickly faded when she saw it was only me.

"Are the others in?"

She didn't answer: her gaze soared above my head

and down the path, and the welcome she flashed was not meant for me. I turned round.

A young man was loping towards her.

He was tall and lean, with hair the colour of pale, dry sand curling down his neck. He wore patched jeans tucked into heavy, knee-high boots and a chunky fisherman's sweater; rather incongruously, he was carrying a leather briefcase.

For a moment his eyes alighted on me with a disconcerting coolness: they were a curious sea-shade of green.

Then Jane squeezed past, ran to meet him and took his hand. I noticed that the dress she had on was good enough for a party.

"Ran!" she beamed. "Oh—look, come in."

We all trooped through the door.

"This your little sister?" He had a clipped, foreign sounding accent that hissed and sizzled over each "s".

"No. Hang on, I'll call her."

She yelled upstairs for Annie. Ran looked quizzically at me. I explained, "I'm Tess. Annie's friend."

"Ah." He nodded; then added with sudden interest, "Tess, you said?"

"Mmm."

"Tess." He repeated it softly to himself as if it reminded him of something. "I see."

"She's coming," said Jane, louder than was necessary. I could tell she was jealous of any claim on his attention: even of little, gawky me!

Annie clattered down.

"Annie, Tess is here for you. And this is Ranulf. Can we borrow your computer for an hour or so please?"

51

Annie stared at the two of them.

"Now? But I thought you were going out, Jane. You're all dressed up."

Jane reddened.

"I'm using the computer at the moment," Annie went on, "so I'm afraid you can't."

"You're only *playing* with it," Jane retorted. "We want it for something urgent. Ran's doing a study. Some very important research."

"Oh yes?" said Annie, folding her arms. "What's this about then?"

"I've just got hold of some new data, you see, Annie," said Ran charmingly. "I'd like to put it through a computer as quickly as possible; but with it being Saturday there's going to be a big delay. Real nuisance! Then Jane told me you have one here. I'm sorry, I didn't realise it belonged to you. Would you mind? It won't take too long."

"What's it about?" persisted Annie. "I'm quite interested in scientific research myself."

"Of course she doesn't mind!" Jane turned to Annie with desperate eyes: "*Please.*"

"Later," said Annie.

"No, *now*. Ran can't wait."

She grabbed his hand and began to lead him up the stairs: Annie and I followed. In the attic we caught her unplugging the computer and lifting it off the desk.

"Put it *back*!" Annie screamed at her.

Jane was sweating with its weight: her make-up started to run.

"Here, let me take it," Ranulf said firmly. In his sinewy arms, the machine seemed to weigh no more than an empty cardboard box. Annie watched, helpless, as he carried it out. We trailed after them.

"Where are you taking it?!"

"Downstairs," said Jane, "to the best room."

"You're not! Mum'll go spare if you get so much as a crumb of dust in there!"

"Look," said Jane, "I can take Ran where I want to, see? Now then, Annie, perhaps you could do a favour and leave us alone!"

On the landing below we heard a door click behind them.

"Well," said Annie, "*well*!" We went back into the attic. "So that's the famous Ranulf! I wonder what they're up to down there."

"Snogging?" I said hopefully. "They couldn't wait to lock the door."

Annie shook her head. "Well, maybe a bit. But he really *did* seem anxious to get his hands on the computer, that's the funny thing."

We got good mileage out of discussing their romance for half an hour or so; then suddenly the front door slammed.

"The parents?" said Annie, looking at her watch. "No, they won't be back until at least half-four. They're out with Oliver and Rob. Maybe it's the lovey-doveys. Maybe they've gone out."

We crept downstairs to see.

The best room door was still shut, but the handle gave when Annie tried it. She switched on the light and we went in.

I'd never been in there before: it was really posh.

There was a long settee and three or four deep armchairs, all covered in flouncy rich material, and the carpet had a thick, deep pile. In the wide bay

53

window with its velvet curtains stood a polished oval dining table. The computer, still switched on, lay on top.

Eight elegant, carved chairs stood around it: the three nearest ones in casual disarray. Ran had left his open brief-case on one of them, covered with a scattering of coloured papers.

"Ahah!" Annie marched resolutely in and began to shuffle through them.

"Annie, don't do that," I said, "they might be private."

"Private my foot! They've got no business to pinch my computer if they don't want me to know what they're up to."

"But supposing they come back and catch us?"

She hesitated. "You'd better wait by the door then, Tess. You'll be able to hear if they come in."

She went back to the papers.

"Hey, this is . . . you'll never guess what he's doing research into!"

"Well?"

"Whales!"

"Wales? What's he come to Shetland for then?"

"No, thicko! *Whales*. Great big mammals that swim in the sea."

"Oh."

"You don't sound very interested."

"Should I be?"

She didn't answer, but went on turning over the pages.

"Come on, Annie. Jane will turn into a raving maniac if she finds us."

"Wow, Tess! Just come here!"

Her stubbornness was starting to infuriate me: I

turned away from the landing for a second to see what on earth she was rabbiting on about.

She thrust a piece of paper into my hand. "Look at this!"

The heading said: *Whale Communication and Echolocation: Preliminary Interpretation Data.* I groaned: did she really expect me to read something as dry and unintelligible as that?

Then the rest of the page caught my eye. It was divided into two columns. On the right hand was a list of English words and phrases.

And on the left, under the heading *Whale Code*, was ranged a curiously familiar pattern of dashes and dots.

# 7

## Symbols and Meanings

The symbols swam before my eyes. The paper was shaking in my hand and my legs seemed turned to jelly. I sat heavily down.

"Whales," I said. "*Whales*."

We heard the front door slam again and two sets of footsteps leaping up the stairs.

"Quick!" cried Annie—but it was too late: they were already creaking across the landing. The door opened and we both froze in mid-flight.

They came in. Ran was carrying something in a stationer's bag. When he saw us there, a curious expression scudded like a cloud across his face.

I was still holding the cryptic sheet of paper. My nervous fingers lost their grip on it and sent it fluttering to the floor.

Without a word, Ran bent to pick it up. He took it over to the computer, pulled up a chair, fished pen and notebook from his shop-bag and resumed work calmly, tapping the keyboard, jotting things down.

"Well," said Annie sheepishly, "we'd better leave you to it."

We began to inch out.

"Tess!" Ran's voice called after us. In the gloom of the landing it made me jump.

"Ignore them," urged Annie.

"Hey there, just a minute!"

Curiosity got the better of me and I went back in, with Annie at my heels.

Ran pushed back his chair and came towards us. His look was dazzling: I could see why Jane was bowled over by him.

"You seem so interested," he said. "Would you like me to show you what I'm doing?"

"Yes," I said in disbelief. "Please."

He led us both to the computer and sent his long, tanned fingers flying over the keyboard. Dots, dashes and squiggles began to appear on the screen.

"You've seen from this, I think," he said, pointing to the paper, "that I'm researching into whales. Well, these symbols show the way they kind of talk to each other, the noises they make. We're just starting to work out what all the different sounds mean.

"I'll show you a quick example, then maybe you'll understand."

He threw me a brief grin that made me glow, reminding me of Mrs MacBride's welcoming smile. "I can get some real good patterns."

My heart jumped at the word 'patterns'. What did he mean? What did he know about whales?

He tapped out another set of symbols.

"Now this here, see, means 'food in this direction'. And that one, we guess it means 'danger'. Of course, it's nothing like this really. When you *hear* the whales talking—well, you got to be real lucky to do that—it sounds like music almost." His watery-deep eyes were studying me. "Like singing."

"Singing?" I repeated weakly.

"That's it. It's pretty fine to hear it, Tess."

"Ran," said Jane pleadingly, "you've shown them

57

now—*surely* that's enough? Can't we have some time to ourselves?"

He shrugged, laughing up at her. "Well, OK."

"Right," she said to us, "go on then—*scram!*"

We did—and met Oliver and Rob coming up the stairs.

"The parents have met an old crony," said Oliver. "We left them to it. They'll be half an hour yet."

"Good," said Annie, "now come up quickly. We've got something amazing to reveal to you."

Back in the attic, we told them about Ranulf and the whales.

Oliver whistled. "Shucks! What idiots we were! That TV programme last year—remember?"

"Yes!" cried Rob. "Whales booming at each other you mean?"

"Uhuh," said Oliver. "They're supposed to be pretty brainy, aren't they? They reckoned on this film, Tess, that they could be going to take over the planet after us."

"Anyway," said Annie, "I'm glad it's solved the mystery. I told you it was something completely logical and ordinary didn't I? But *now* what's the matter, Tess?"

"Ordinary?" I said. "Can . . . can you hear them on the land though? Surely not. Surely you could only hear the noises they make under the sea?"

"I'd have thought that's obvious," said Rob.

"Then how come that *I*'ve heard them?"

There was a long pause.

"Ahah," said Oliver, polishing his glasses, "the mystery thickens, after all."

"And Miss Tait," I said, "she told me it was a warning. A message . . ."

59

"This is getting daft!" cried Annie. "Apart from anything else, if whales were really bright enough to go round sending messages, surely they'd realise that humans can't understand them."

"Has anyone," said Oliver, "got any ideas?"

I closed my eyes and willed the image of a tiny golden key into my mind. *I must work this out, I must.* Thoughts swam into view.

"I think . . . I might have a clue."

"Go on."

"It might be like this." The thoughts grew bigger, surer as I spoke them.

"Well, you know how they've sent rockets into outer space—right out of the solar system? And then they've buried time-capsule things, to be dug out of the earth in, say, two, three thousand years' time. They put messages in them, don't they?—in the hope that someone, somewhere, in some other time, might find them. But of course, these people—or things—probably won't understand English. So they put the message into a code-language—a sort of Maths-language, isn't it Annie?—so that anyone—any-thing—that finds it, if they're intelligent enough, might be able to make sense of what it's about."

"I'm beginning to see what you're getting at," said Annie.

"So this," I said, "might be the same thing."

"A cross-species code?" said Oliver. "Something so simple that even us super-thick humans can under-stand it—once we've worked out how to crack it."

"And someone's already done *that* for us," said Rob. "The famous Ranulf!"

The attic door suddenly opened and Jane poked her head round.

"I'm going out with Ran. Tell the parents I'll be back in time for supper."

Oliver blinked at her slyly.

"Make sure you're a good girl."

She glared stonily back at him. Through the crack we could see Ran hovering in the background. As if he'd prompted her, she added with false sweetness, "Oh, and thank you for the use of the computer, Annie."

Then she was gone and we heard them scuttling downstairs and out. We waited, dead still, for a couple of minutes; then Annie said, "Oliver, help us lug the computer back up here, will you?"

Rob and I went down with them to the best room.

"Typical!" moaned Annie when we got there. "She's even too lazy to turn it off."

She moved her hand to the switch, but Rob suddenly stayed her.

"Hang on, what's *that*?"

The screen was flickering. Annie shook Rob off and twiddled agitatedly with some knobs until the image cleared.

"It's the code! He's left his whale-code program in the computer!"

I stared at it. A tight, jumpy feeling that had been tying itself into my stomach sealed its last, steely knot. I wondered if I'd ever feel safe and normal again.

"Why?" I whispered. "*Why?*"

"What's it matter?" cried Annie. "Now we can translate your noises at last!"

From downstairs, we heard a commotion of people coming in, of bags and boxes thumping into the hall; and then the bell rang.

"The parents are back," said Oliver. "We'd better clear up in here fast."

"And now that sounds like my mum," I said. "I'm afraid I've got to go."

I helped them straighten up the best room and get the computer back into its proper place, while the adults made small-talk down below.

"Ring us tonight," said Oliver, "so as we can tell you if we've found anything."

But later, after supper, with Mum and Dad dozing on and off in front of the telly, it seemed there was no chance of having a private chat on the phone. And the way things were turning out, I daren't risk them hearing anything—not even a whisper—of what was going on.

I remembered there was a public call-box about a mile down the lonely road. We'd used it once or twice when our own phone had been out of order. So I said I was taking Freya out, stuffed a few ten pences into my pocket, and stepped into the night.

It was clear and crisp and cold. A full moon lit the track. I wrapped a scarf tightly round my head and broke into a run to keep warm.

Freya barked happily, exhilarated by the moonlight, wanting to play.

We reached the phone-box. Freya squeezed in too, and crouched between my legs. I dialled the Sinclairs' number, feeling a sense of unreality: the phone-box was a tiny island of civilisation in an emptiness of moorland and night.

Oliver answered.

"Hello, it's me. Has Annie worked anything out yet?"

"Yup!"

In the background, I heard a sudden whooping noise.

"Tess, that's Annie now! She's got something to tell us. Oh . . . Hello? Can you hang on for a couple of minutes?"

He disappeared before I could answer. I waited; the pips went: you didn't get long for your money.

I hung up and decided to count up to two hundred before I rang them again.

But of course, their end was still off the hook. They didn't know where I was, they couldn't ring me back.

I dialled the number, over and over, cursing, shuddering with the seeping cold, while Freya began to whine.

Then at last I got through. I heard Annie's voice: "Tess? Oh thank goodness, we thought we'd lost you. Now listen, we've put your Singing through the computer and guess what, it really does seem to make some sense!"

"Go on then."

"Mind you, it's a bit odd. But perhaps you might have more idea than us of what it means."

"What *is* it?"

"Remember, it sounds rather stilted because it's all in sort of 'key-words' from Ranulf's code"

"For goodness sake, Annie, tell me what it says!"

"I'll read it to you then."

She cleared her throat.

"It says, *danger—obstruction—towards land—moving—obstruction — approaching — danger — danger — danger*. Then there's a sort of squiggly thing that we can't work out. But it's the last bit that's most peculiar.

"It says: *attack—towards land—attack—attack—attack*."

63

# 8

## *Who* Are *You?"*

It was my turn to have the others to stay for a
weekend. I persuaded Mum to put up the boys as
well as Annie: they brought sleeping-bags and settled
down in the old box-room that we never normally
use.

First thing after breakfast, they all wanted to meet
Miss Tait. Mum gave us some goodies for her, and
with Freya bounding at our heels we set off.

It was a fresh, wind-whipped morning.

Having the others there gave me confidence. I
banged loudly on the peeling door.

We had to wait a couple of minutes; and then
Jacobina Tait flung it open. Rob gasped. Her white
hair, unbrushed and unbound, stuck out round her
shoulders like a tangled sheep's fleece, and she was
wearing an ancient blue dressing-gown. She had a
man's slippers on her feet.

"What do you want?" she yapped, glaring above
our heads. "It's too early for callers!"

Freya began to whine and rub herself round my
knees. Miss Tait glance down.

"Oh, that wretched dog again!"

Then suddenly she recognised me.

"Ah, Teresa. But who are these ragamuffins?"

Rob stifled a snigger.

"We've brought some eggs for you, Miss Tait,"
said Oliver politely.

"I'm not dressed yet. Wait out here until I am."

She closed the door abruptly and we looked around for somewhere to wait. Oliver pointed through the jungle of weeds and spiders' webs glinting with dew to her little boat.

"We could sit on that."

So we hacked a way through and perched gingerly on its side. I'd always thought it must be completely rotten with age and disuse, but when we came to it, the boat looked surprisingly sea-worthy under its dry, white crust of barnacles.

Rob said, "She's better than I ever imagined! A riot!"

The door opened again without us hearing it, and Miss Tait's voice bellowed: "Get off there at once!"

We jumped up guiltily.

"All right, you can come in now."

Inside, her cluttered room smelt damp and chilly.

"Is it all right if we sit down please?" asked Annie.

"Of course it's all right!" Her voice softened, though her manner stayed brusque and nervy: perhaps she wasn't used to seeing so many people at once. "You've no need to stand to attention."

I could see the others trying not to laugh.

"I don't know what you want of me," Miss Tait said. "I can't offer you tea, because my fire's not lit yet, so the kettle can't be boiled."

"Would you like me to do the fire?" offered Oliver.

She relaxed a bit at that: "Thank you—you've got some manners then."

"Where do you keep the coal?"

"Peats!" she snapped at him.

"Peats, then?"

"In the shed round the back. You'll find paper and sticks there too. You're a good boy."

She watched him while he cleaned the grate and carefully laid the tinders.

"Manners . . ." she turned suddenly on Annie and Rob ". . . but you haven't even got that! *I* know why you've come!"

They were transfixed by her.

"You want to know what's going on, don't you? Eh? You're nosey-parkers, that's what you are!"

"Please, Miss Tait, they're my friends," I said.

Oliver put a match to the fire: it sent yellow flames leaping up.

"Well then," she went on, "are you deaf, you three ragamuffins? How much do you know? Can you hear it?"

"What?" said Rob indignantly.

"The Singing."

"We've never tried," said Annie, in a small voice.

"Then it's time you did." Miss Tait hobbled to the door, opened it and sniffed the wind. "Yes, it's right. It should come to you now. Out you get!"

"What do you mean?" said Rob.

"*The Singing*—I want to know which of you can hear it."

She shooed us out: her sunken gaze sent us off, unquestioningly obedient, up across the short, wiry grass towards the nearest cliff.

"Hey," said Annie suddenly, "what's up with Freya?"

Ahead of us, the dog had stopped. She was half sitting, her tail wedged firmly between her legs, hackles risen, stiff and panting; every so often she let out a strangled little whimper.

Dread stabbed me. I stopped too, and listened.

And the Singing floated in, sweet and haunting as a dream.

Whenever I heard it, all my senses were sharpened. I became very aware of myself, standing there in the bitter cold, perhaps fifty metres from the water's edge.

One of the others—I wasn't sure which—said, "What's wrong, Tess?"

The Singing was growing louder. It seemed to fill the whole ocean and sky.

My speech came out drunken-slow and bleary: "Can't *you* hear it?"

"No," said Annie.

"No," said Oliver.

"No," said Rob.

It wasn't a misty day this time. The air was crisp and diamond-clean. The breeze, though it cut raw against the skin, was almost silent.

I could hear the Singing clearer than I'd ever done before.

"Freya can hear something too," said Annie, "that's obvious. But we can't."

"It's for me," I said wanly. "The whales are singing for me."

I walked on, like a sleep-walker. When I was almost at the cliff's edge, I felt Oliver grab me firmly by the arm; otherwise I might well have gone further and tumbled right over.

I knew that they were there. My heart went out to them and I longed to make some answer.

"Come on," said Oliver gently. "You look awful Tess. Let's go."

I suppose it would have been safer, more sensible

to go home, but without even discussing it, we all automatically turned to Miss Tait's house.

She was waiting for us with cups of something steaming, sweet, dark purple.

"Mulled blackberry juice," she said. "It'll warm you up."

We all swallowed it and I felt surprisingly better. Indoors, I couldn't hear anything except for the peat-fire roaring, Freya breathing into a relieved sleep and our own normal conversation.

There weren't enough chairs for five. Miss Tait made us all sit down, while she herself stood by the stove, leaning on her thick drift-wood stick.

"Well?"

"The others couldn't hear it, Miss Tait," I said.

"And what does that tell you?"

I hesitated.

"Maybe . . . I've got some extra special sense?"

"You're flattering yourself, Teresa. Think!"

"Or maybe . . . maybe the Singing's only *aimed* at me."

"Exactly! The whales are singing to *you*, Teresa. Now then."

I started. She'd known all along it was the whales!

"Miss Tait," I said slowly, "I wrote the Singing down. We found a code, and Annie here fed it through her computer. This is what it seemed to say." I recited the eerie message: we all knew it now by heart. "What does it *mean*?"

"What do *you* think it means? It's not for me to tell you."

I said: "I've been thinking." I swallowed. "'Danger'. 'A moving obstruction' in the sea. Well

. . ." I heard my voice falter to a hoarse whisper. "Could it be—something like an *oil slick?*"

"Ach!" She leapt up, her ancient eyes sparkling with a strange, liquid fire: involuntarily I shrank back.

"And your father—?"

"*My father?*"

"That's why they're calling to *you* Teresa! They know him as a wicked, evil man! They're trying to reach *him*, through you!"

I opened my mouth to contradict her, but no words came.

"Oh no, you *won't* deny it! He's turning the sea into a sticky, deathly mess of black drifting oil. It is true, Teresa, isn't it, eh? Well *they* know what's going on, that's for certain. They know the one who's behind it all!"

My father? Never in my wildest anger had I thought of him like that before! Evil? My dad? I couldn't grasp it. He was a right laugh, wasn't he, my dad, when he wasn't too busy . . .

Thoughts chased through my mind. *Why* was he so busy all the time then? What was he up to? *But I love my dad.* Don't I? But what about the papers I'd seen on his desk; why was he so evasive when I asked about his work?

"How do they know? How do *you* know?"

She threw the question back at me: "Are they right about your father?"

"I . . . I'm not sure. Perhaps . . . I discovered something—by accident—perhaps I understood it wrong. I shouldn't have seen it anyway." I remembered the bright red warning printed on top of the circular letter. "It's secret. Top secret."

"And so is this."

Miss Tait shuffled to a door in the wall to the right of the stove—the one she wouldn't open in front of me the other time I was there.

"I think it is time for me to show you into my back room."

She fetched the miniature laquered cabinet from its shelf and handed it to me.

"Open it please, Teresa. You know now how to find the key."

Oliver clucked admiringly as, without hesitation, I pressed open the secret compartment, pulled out tiny box after tiny box, and came at last to the key.

Miss Tait fitted it into a lock as small as the key was, and pushed open the door. Within, it seemed there was no window: just a musty darkness. She lit two oil lamps and carried them through.

"You can come in now."

We followed her into a mess of dust and jumble. Old cardboard boxes were piled from floor to ceiling. The room was a narrow oblong; against the longest wall stood a rickety trestle-table, covered with a tangle of papers and fragments of knitting.

The knitting was all Fair Isle patterns, really complicated ones in loads of different colours: dismembered backs, sleeves and yokes—in the shadowy lamplight, I couldn't see any finished garments.

"Did you do these?" I asked stupidly.

"Yes. I suppose you didn't know I could? Well then, now I shall tell you about the patterns. These for example," she said, holding up one of the Fair Isles. "It's all part of a code of course. The message is knitted into the pattern. I send them to Mrs

MacBride's shop, and she passes them on. It all looks so innocent."

"Passes them—?"

"To the others. To those of us in league. There are more of us than you might realise. But we have to move secretly: it isn't an easy task."

There was a long silence. Miss Tait waited.

"Who *are* you?" I asked, at last.

"You might call us . . . guardians. We come and go, like the tide. We watch and pass on messages. Sometimes we reveal ourselves when there are especially difficult tasks we have to do."

Rob hunched his shoulders and shoved his hands into his pockets.

"What are you guarding? Who are you passing messages to? How do we know you're not just making it up?"

"She's not making up the Singing," I answered for her.

"You see here," said Miss Tait, "I have stored many thousands of code messages like this. They have been coming in to me over the years, while the oil danger has been gathering. If you can understand all this, you will realise also that there are many, many codes, everywhere. Look for the patterns. You will often find them in quite ordinary people and places."

"But who are you working for?" demanded Rob. "There must be . . ."

"Will you be satisfied if I tell you it is all for the power of good?" said Miss Tait. "There are mysteries beyond your understanding, young man; but there is nothing to be afraid of. Everything starts and ends with the sea."

"But my *father*?" I asked again, biting my lip, "what about my dad?"

"They're going to stop this oil catastrophe, by hook or by crook," said Miss Tait. "We have sent the messages on to the whales. In their wisdom, they understand the ones they must try and reach. They have chosen you, Teresa, as the direct channel to your father."

"But it's not just my dad!" I almost screamed at her, "it's the whole oil company! Why pick on me?"

". . . Your privelege," Miss Tait was murmuring, "to hear the Singing . . ."

"I don't *want* to hear it though! I wish I never had!"

". . . and your burden, to end your father's evil."

There was a silence. I was fighting back tears.

"So now," said Miss Tait, as if we had come to the end of something, "you understand it a little, at least."

She ushered us back through the door, blew out the lamps and locked it firmly behind her.

"But can I be sure of you all? Teresa has already invited in you others without my consent. Perhaps it was a good thing. *But this must not go beyond your knowledge.*"

"We've already sworn an oath," said Rob, and even his voice was trembling now, "of secrecy. Signed in blood."

She peered at us deeply, one by one.

"That's good. I believe I can trust you. You know, of course, that Mrs MacBride is one of us, but even to her you mustn't let on. As for the others—you will see them, perhaps, if you use your eyes and ears . . ."

And then suddenly, imperceptibly, something in

73

Miss Tait's manner changed. A shutter went down; the breath of weirdness went out of her; she was just a wrinkled, rather grubby old lady, ordinary and matter of fact.

"Thank you for coming to see me. And thank your mother, Teresa, for the eggs."

But as we were setting off for home, she called me back.

"Teresa, you're taking this very well you know."

She took my hand; and her grip was so light that I scarcely knew it was there.

I couldn't think of how to answer: "Miss Tait . . ."

"You can call me Jacobina if you like," she said, "if it makes us seem more like friends."

She smiled with unexpected warmth: I met her sunken eyes, and even they were smiling too. The fear melted from my heart, and instead I felt a sadness I couldn't explain.

"Despite everything, I hope you'll remember me as a friend," said Jacobina. "And now you must be on your way, do what you've got to do to rid us of this evil, do it well and carefully—and you and I must say goodbye."

It wasn't until much later that I understood the finality of that parting.

# 9

# *Fighting*

Dad had been working at the terminal all day; he came in late as usual and it was nearly seven o'clock before we could all sit down to eat. By now, his harrassed expression had hardened into an unchanging mask; still, he made an effort to be friendly to Annie and the others.

"Had a good day?" he asked.

Oliver nodded. "We've been walking on the cliffs. It's nice to get out."

"Yes," said Dad, "you're a bit hemmed in, aren't you, living in Lerwick."

"Oh, we like it," said Annie. "There's always things happening there."

"Like Up-Helly-Aa," said Rob.

"Ah," said Dad, "well, it looks like *I* won't have time to get there this year. I suppose you'll be wanting to see it though, Tess?"

Up-Helly-Aa is the great Shetland fire festival when they burn a Viking longship and have music, acting and processions. It's a fantastic event: a dazzle of brightness in midwinter: it happens every year at the end of January and goes on half the night.

Mum said, "Surely you won't still be working evenings by then will you, love?"

Dad grunted. "It looks like it. If we don't find a solution by Christmas there's no knowing . . ."

Their eyes met, and abruptly they let the matter drop.

Annie said, "Mrs Jamieson, Tess could come to the festival with us, if she'd like to."

"We'll see," said Mum.

We cleared away, and the Sinclairs earned their keep by helping with the washing-up. There weren't enough tea-towels to go round: Dad and I were superfluous. We joined in the chit-chat for a while, and then I followed him out of the kitchen.

I took a deep breath.

"Dad—could I have a word with you?"

"'Course you can. What's up, Tess?"

"Could we go into your study? It's . . . private."

We went in and shut the door behind us.

"Well?"

It was hard to know how to begin.

"Dad—this oil . . ."

He raised his eyebrows at me.

"I know more about what's going on than you think."

For a few seconds he stood there, staring at me intently. I was scared he was going to lose his temper, but all he said was, "You're a bright girl, aren't you Tess? Sharp. Quick on the uptake." He wasn't being sarcastic. "Well then, you'd better explain exactly what this is all about."

"One thing—I know it's secret," I said quickly. "I haven't told anyone else, Dad, not even Annie. I promise."

"OK, I believe you. Carry on."

I perched uncomfortably on a corner of his desk, trying hard to meet him on his own level. It wasn't easy. I had a sudden flash of how awful it must be to carry all that responsibility on your shoulders.

"I saw it here. On your desk."

"You saw—?"

"The notice. The warning. This emergency—there's an oil slick coming out already isn't there? A dreadful big one. It's going to pollute the sea."

He let out a deep sigh and nodded.

"But *surely* you're not just going to let it happen?"

He hesitated, choosing his words with care.

"Unfortunately, there are others above me, Tess. I have to act on instructions."

"*Whose* instructions?"

"The Board of Directors, for a start."

"But you've always said you're your own boss!"

"For day to day running the show, yes. But these are . . . rather unusual circumstances, Tess. There's so much money tied up in it—millions of pounds, to be quite frank with you—that some of the chaps reckon it's not worth . . ."

"Not worth clearing up the oil? How can they say that? How can *you* say that?"

"I haven't said anything." He sighed again. "It's just that in this game you have to weigh the odds one against the other. It's not so easy to decide . . ."

"You mean your bosses couldn't care less if the company pollutes the sea? Dad, how *can* you let this happen?!"

"How can I stop them, Tess, that's the thing? They reckon the cost of clearing up the mess afterwards is nothing to the setbacks of shutting down the new system now it's almost underway."

I tried to interrupt.

"No—*listen* to me, Tess, wait till I've finished. I

*have* told them what I think, believe me. They're quite aware and concerned about the effect it'll have on the sea round Shetland. In fact, they went off and commissioned an expert to do some calculations on exactly what might happen. At the very worst, she reckoned, so many thousands of fish will die, and so many hundreds of birds—but then, she says, the numbers should be made up again and recovered within about five years. The Board feels that five years isn't that long to wait in overall conservation terms—not when you look at how much this new system could do for jobs and getting everyone richer right across the islands. They've promised donations to the Island Council and they'll help any environmental groups involved in clearing up the mess. So— as far as they're concerned, everything's all right."

I tried anxiously to read his face.

"But it isn't all right really, is it?"

"Not by me it isn't, no."

I said, "Then how can you carry on with it?"

" 'Ours is not to reason why, ours is just to do and die'."

"*Die*? Dad, what do you mean—?"

He laughed hollowly.

"It's only a quote, Tess. What I mean is, sometimes in life you have to learn to do what you're told— despite what your better judgement tells you."

"No! You can't just sit back and take orders! You've got to rebel—" I slid off the desk and ran to him. "Go on strike! You've got to refuse to send any more of this dreadful oil into the sea!"

"And do you know what'll happen if I do that? They'll sling me out on my ear, Tess, give me the sack. *Phut*! Just like that."

"Not someone as important as you!"

"Oh, there's plenty more where I came from."

"Then . . . but you've got to take the risk!"

"It's not a risk," Dad said dryly, "it's a certainty. Can you imagine what it's like to lose your job, Tess, eh? There's no other work I could do up here. Do you think I want to subject you and Mum to all the problems that would bring?"

"But there *is* other work! You could campaign, Dad. You could work to stop any more pollution. That would be a really good thing to do—much better than what you do now."

"Oh, it would indeed. But who do you think is going to pay me to do it?"

"I . . . I don't know."

"Then what would we live on?"

"Mum could work. I don't know how she can bear just being a housewife. She could get more chickens and sell the eggs. She could get some goats or cows and make cheese to sell. She could get a *proper* job—in an office or something."

"You don't know what you're talking about."

"I *do*!"

"You don't. There are no opportunities here. If I lost my job, we'd have to leave Shetland, move to one of the cities down south."

He threw the idea at me like an accusation.

"I don't *care*!" I threw back at him. "That's in the future. What matters is *now*—saving the sea. Saving the fish and the birds and the whales . . ."

"Whales?" he said, suddenly distracted, "no that's something I don't think we need worry about. Haven't seen any whales off this coast since back past last summer."

"There are! I know there are!"

"Yes, yes," he said wearily, "you know everything don't you? All right Tess, I won't argue with you any more. I've tried to talk to you like an adult—perhaps it was a mistake."

"I'm sorry," I whispered, "about snooping at your papers, I mean."

"OK, OK, forget it."

He strode over to the door.

"But Dad—" I grabbed his arm in desperation, but he wrenched it from me and opened the door.

"You've got to understand this," he said. "When I'm home I just want to switch off, forget about my work. Now leave me a little peace, to enjoy the evening and relax, eh?"

There was a strange catch in his voice, a sort of breaking; but it was the force with which he pulled away which shook me. Bleakly I watched him walk back into the kitchen.

It wrecked the rest of the evening. Anyway, we had to be polite to my parents and sit demurely in the living room playing Monopoly with them. My heart wasn't in it, and I was the first one out.

I slipped off to take Freya for her evening run, then upstairs to get ready for bed.

And all the time I was thinking about Dad.

It was like I'd seen through him. All right then, perhaps he did genuinely care about the pollution— but in that case, why was he too weak and feeble to stick up for his beliefs?

I knew what *I* would do in his position—I'd go straight to those rotten directors and tell them I was going to disobey their orders, and then I'd go right off and shut down the whole new system. I'd start an uprising—a revolution—right through the company, get everyone to support me. *I* wouldn't be scared to stick my neck out—how else can you make things better in the world? But Dad—what a let down!—he just didn't have the guts.

A weak and gutless father—fancy being stuck with someone like that! But even worse, supposing he hadn't been honest with me after all? Supposing when it came down to it, *he* didn't really care about the pollution either?

My stomach went all cold.

*Wicked*, Miss Tait had said, *evil*.

Evil? My dad? I shivered: it wasn't a nice thought.

Annie came up: she was going to sleep on the camp-bed in my room.

"Rob won," she said in disgust.

"Hard luck."

"Tess, are you listening?"

I climbed into bed and turned out the light.

"Yes," I lied.

"I'm thinking of working out on my computer the average chance any one player has of winning at Monopoly. But you'll have to help me gather facts for the program."

"For goodness sake, Annie, you know I can't understand all this maths talk! Pack it in, won't you. I need to get to sleep."

"Well! And after you've invited me here! Why are you in such a huff? It's always the best bit, talking in bed."

"Not now," I muttered. "Just leave me."

"Tess," said Annie, "something's wrong."

"No."

81

"It is, your voice has gone all weepy. Is it to do with when you went off before with your dad?"

"No."

The camp bed creaked as she sat down heavily on the edge.

"Tell us," she said. "Don't bottle it up."

I sniffed and tried to sound steady.

"OK," I said at last, "Yes, it's Dad."

She began brushing her hair, over and over, to fill in the silence.

"And to do with what Miss Tait said," I went on, "but of course, you gathered that."

"Yes."

"Annie, this is awful. My dad's partly in charge of making this oil slick that the whales are sending messages about."

"So it's true!"

"I had it out with him, Annie, but it's like talking to a brick wall! He's either too spineless to stick up for what's right—or else he doesn't even care. And if he doesn't care, what's worse is he *lied* to me by pretending that he does."

She grunted sympathetically.

Huddled over the sheets, staring into the dark, I let the next words that had slowly been forming rise, unbidden, in my throat. My heart lurched as I spoke them: "I'm beginning to think I hate him, Annie."

"Tess! You mustn't say that sort of thing!"

But in the darkness, memories of our conversation, and of what had passed with Miss Tait, jostled through my mind like demons.

"I hate him," I said again.

It was a spell, a charm, final, harsh and satisfying.

Annie leaned towards me. "Take it back, Tess,"

she pleaded. "That's a terrible thing to say! You've got to take it back."

"I can't, I can't!" I was pinned down, caged, by the enormity of what was happening all around. "I've got to hate him, to save the whales!"

"You must try to take this whole business more calmly," said Annie.

But it wasn't *her* that the whales were calling to.

We went to sleep then, and my dreams were full of treachery and betrayal.

Next morning, we all went over the hill, the opposite way from the cliffs, to a place I knew where you could sit on rabbit-cropped grass behind some rocks, out of view of our house, and beyond the path of the wind.

We held a sort of war council.

I filled the boys in about what had passed between me and Dad.

"I tried to stop him, I really did my utmost to make him see sense and save him from the whales' attack, but it was a complete, useless waste of time. I'm just so scared now that something awful's going to happen."

"Can't *we* stop this oil slick in any way?" said Rob. "On our own?"

"And how, tell me," said Annie. "You can bet the whole system's so complex, not even Einstein could take it to pieces."

"You don't reckon we could sabotage it then?" suggested Rob hopefully.

"Don't be childish—how? Anyway, we'd all end up in prison."

"Perhaps," I said slowly, "we could try and save things the other way round. Go back to the whales.

Tell them we can't stop it. Beg them not to attack—
or not until we've had time to think up some other
way of stopping the oil."

"OK then," said Oliver, "but that sounds even
*more* impossible. How are you going to contact the
whales? There's only Miss Tait, and I can't imagine,
from what she said, that she'd do it for you. Have
you invented some magic way of talking to the whales,
Tess?"

I said, "There's Ranulf."

They all stared at me.

"He's involved with whales."

"But not like that," said Annie. "He's studying
them, that's all."

"He had the Code."

"Lucky coincidence," said Oliver.

In our little stone-bound hollow, the world was
shut out. Nothing intruded. I looked round at the
others.

"He seemed to . . . recognise me," I whispered.

"Now hang on," said Annie, "you're not seriously
suggesting that he's . . ."

"A guardian? Yes."

"Jane's boyfriend?" guffawed Rob. "Blimey, no!"

"Annie," I said, "you saw how he was to me. How
he seemed to be sort of . . . leading me on."

She considered. "Well, I must admit, he did seem
rather anxious to show you things."

"Can't we ask him then?"

"Well, I suppose we could. We'll have to be careful
though."

She looked seriously round at her brothers.

"It sounds ridiculous, but I reckon there could be
just a chance . . . Especially after what Miss Tait

84

said about recognising patterns and guardians and things."

I could hear the doubt in her voice, but generously she pushed it away.

"It's a long shot—but worth a try. But of course, whether we can actually get hold of Ranulf again— that all depends on Jane."

# 10

# A Meeting in the Dark

"Going somewhere nice?" asked Annie.

She and I were sitting in a corner of the attic, watching Jane getting ready to go out. And Jane stood by the full-length mirror, twirling round to admire herself, her golden hair gleaming.

"I hope so."

"With Ran?"

"Uhuh."

"You must know him quite well by now."

Jane sighed. "He doesn't have much time to take me out."

Annie got up and went over to brush an invisible speck of dust off her sister's shoulders. "I expect his research takes up quite a bit of time?"

"Mmmm. It seems to."

"It sounds ever so interesting though, what he's doing. You look lovely, Jane."

"Thanks."

"I'd like to ask him more about it some time."

"What?"

"Whales."

"Huh?"

"His research. You know I want to get on in science. Do you think I could have a chat with him about it some time—and Tess too?"

"No," said Jane.

"Perhaps if you bring him back here for coffee? Or when he calls round for you?"

"No."

Annie looked at me. I had a flash of inspiration.

"We've just started a project in biology, you see," I said. "About whales. We thought he could help us. It's . . . we've got to finish it quickly. It's sort of urgent. If we could do something really good before the end of term—and he could help us—it wouldn't take long."

"Tess," said Jane, "you're not having me on?"

"Of course not."

"Then tell me exactly what you need to know, and if he's in the right mood, I'll ask him about it."

"I . . . I can't really," I said. "It's . . . too complicated."

"Then forget it."

"But you see . . ." said Annie.

"For goodness' sake, you'll make me late!"

Jane grabbed handbag, coat, took one last look in the mirror, and went flurrying out of the room.

I watched her disappear in a haze of swinging hair and scent. An idea took root in my mind. Did I dare? Did Annie dare?

"Annie," I said, "get your coat. "Let's follow her. Follow *them*. Catch the famous Ranulf for ourselves."

I wasn't sure how she'd respond: she thinks everything through, slowly and sensibly, does Annie.

"Are you coming? Make up your mind, quick."

She pursed her lips, then grinned at me: "OK." She laughed. "Yes—why not!"

We ran downstairs, pulling on outdoor things as we went, and crept out the front door. Jane had a good head-start: we stood helplessly in the street, not able to see her at first. If she was catching a bus out of town, we'd have to let her go. But then we caught sight of her, walking quickly towards one of the steep, narrow lanes that led down to the centre of town.

We shadowed her, hoods up, keeping our distance, melting into walls and gateways. Down the lane she went, where the thin lamps could scarcely penetrate the night gloom. Half way along she stopped, and waited by a door.

Ran came strolling up. He didn't wear a coat, although the night was frosty. We peered furtively round a corner: even through the darkness, you could see the colour of his eyes, a strange, shining green. He took her hand and led her through the lighted doorway, down some stairs.

"Where are they going?"

"Folk-club I think," said Annie. "It's in a basement."

"Can we get in?"

"We could try."

"Like this?" We were wearing jeans and our school duffle-coats to keep out the cold.

"Doesn't matter what you wear—only your age. Push your hair back, Tess, it makes you look older. That's better. Now—follow me."

Inside, a red light-bulb disguised us in its dim glow. The man on the door was young and dreamy: we paid our entrance and he scarcely gave us a glance.

"Where are they? She mustn't see us."

We stood nervously outside the main room, pressed against the wall. Other people came in, talking and laughing: the air grew heavy with cigarette smoke and the stale smell of beer. I began to feel uneasy.

Most of the people were Ran's age, the men rugged, the girls dressed like gypsies. I began to wish that we hadn't come.

"There!" hissed Annie. "Sitting against the wall."

"Do you think they've seen us?"

"Not Jane! She can't take her eyes off him."

"But Ranulf?"

We watched them for a few moments.

"He seems to keep looking this way."

"But has he *seen* us, Annie?"

"I'm not sure."

The music started: a girl sang sombrely and plucked a guitar. We stayed where we were, watching.

"Don't think much of this," said Annie. "If we can't nab him soon, Tess, let's go home."

A load of people squeezed past us and made a great commotion finding seats. We lost sight of Ran until they were settled; and then, when the view was cleared, he was gone.

"Oh," a man's voice said suddenly from behind us, "you wait for the next ones—they play real fine music."

I jumped.

"Annie—that was him!"

"Where'd he go?"

We looked quickly round.

"That way, I think. It looks like there's a sort of bar through there."

We crept through a low arch that led into another half-lit room. Ran was in a crowd fetching drinks from a long counter. A group of boys, about Jane's age, lounging in the doorway, eyed us with leering interest. I began to edge out.

"Annie, it's awful in here. Let's go."

"Don't be daft—come on, now's your chance."

"I'd rather not—I'm sorry . . ."

The stuffiness was closing in on me.

"What—after we've wasted all our pocket-money to get in here! Well, if you won't ask him, *I* jolly well will!"

She marched in. I daren't be left there alone, so I followed lamely. We squeezed through the crush and she touched his arm.

"Ran—"

"Hi." There was not a grain of surprise in his greeting.

"Ran," said Annie, "we wanted to ask you something. Um—about your research."

"Oh yes?"

He came from the bar, carrying two half-pints of sour, frothing beer, and let us trail after him.

"Do you think you could possibly help us?"

He stopped and looked down at us, one by one.

"You Annie? No, I don't think I need to help you. But Tess, now: ah, Tess." He narrowed his eyes at me. "Yes, now maybe I've got to help Tess. Or maybe you got something to tell me? I just hope it's good news, that's all."

I found myself stammering: "I . . . I . . . how do I know I can . . . can trust you?"

"You're right. You got to be careful. You got to be sure of your trust. So I just ask you to wait a little longer—for the next music. I know you're good at listening, Tess. Perhaps you'll hear something in the music, huh?"

His face was awash with secrets.

"Something that you recognise—like a password.

91

And then, if you're ready, you can come and we can talk about the things that we must."

He sidled off, calling back over his shoulder: "Don't worry about your sister, Annie—I'll make sure she doesn't know that you're here."

We trusted him with that at least, Jane seemed so besotted with him. And so we went and sat on some chairs near the doorway of the main room, until by and by, the fiddlers came on.

There were three of them: I don't recall much of what they looked like: only that they held their bows aloft, and then the basement exploded into a carousel of sound.

The music skimmed off their strings like strands of quicksilver, it danced across the room fast and restless like sunlight dappling on and off the water, flickering more quickly than a storm-wind. It seemed to suck us into it, this music, this wordless, formless singing . . .

And the breath went out of me. For the fiddle-music seemed indeed like singing—a distant, unknown Singing. I fought and fought it back but still it came to me: there were patterns in the music. I heard long notes and short ones—

A password, he had said. A password in the music. By that I would know that I could trust him. And Mrs MacBride's words came floating back: *Tell her, they've come.*

"Annie," I said tremulously, "I think I know what he's talking about. I think—I'm sure—he's one of Them."

She nodded, as if she too had some inkling of the patterns.

"Stay with me," I begged her. "Come and keep me safe."

92

We got up and gazed across the room. We could see Jane, enrapt by the fiddlers, but she was alone.

"Perhaps he's waiting for us."

He was, at the top of the stairs, in the quiet, dark street. What danger was I playing with, meeting a man in a lonely back alley? But the fear in me was more than that: I can't describe it.

I grabbed Annie's hand and she stayed there with me, warm and solid, but silent.

He said, "Well Tess. The whales. The oil. Disaster coming. It's not a pretty pattern we find ourselves in."

I could scarcely speak.

He said, "You understand the Singing. We know your father controls the oil. What are we to do?"

"I've spoken to my dad," I said. "I've tried to stop him—I've begged him. He won't listen."

Silently, he watched me.

"What else can I *do*?" My voice was starting to break. "It's not my fault—*I* don't know anything about oil!"

His sea-cold gaze was like an accusation. I heard myself falter into a low, hoarse scream: "Why *me*? Why are you all blaming me?"

Ranulf said gently, "Do you know what I am?"

A strange echo of water seemed everywhere, surging through the lamplight.

I said: "Jacobina told us—the guardians?"

"Yes," he said, "and now the watching and waiting is nearly over. If the messages have failed, I think it will soon be time to act. You must understand this Tess: we don't *want* to harm your father, and this is why we tried to reach him first, through you. But we

93

must keep the oil from destroying the ocean. If we have to use force—what other way is there?"

I felt my heart would wrench in two.

He said, "If the oil keeps leaking, soon many whales will die. Try and imagine the size of a whale's anger! That is why I, and the others, have come."

"But Ranulf," I whispered, "what are all these dreadful things that keep being hinted at? What's going to happen?"

"Ah, the great anger!"

"Tell me," I pleaded, "oh tell me!"

"Go home," said Ranulf. "Things have grown worse than they should be. There's danger in cracks and corners. Stay with your friends, keep from the cliffs, stay ignorant and safe."

And then he was gone, and I found myself with Annie, hurrying back up the lane, into the broad familiar street and back to her brightly lit house.

Her parents were entertaining: we crept in unnoticed. Holding our breath, we leapt upstairs and flung ourselves into the attic.

Oliver and Rob were waiting for us there.

"Where have you been?" demanded Rob.

We looked at each other.

"Forget it," said Oliver impatiently. "Just sit down and listen."

"Don't boss . . ." snapped Annie.

"Shut up!" cried Rob. "Something dreadful's happened."

In a dream still, I took off my coat and sank wearily to the floor.

"It's just come on the radio," said Oliver. "There's a whole mass of whales—"

"*What?*"

94

"They've come in to Yell Sound on the tail of an oil-slick . . ."

"What do you mean?"

"They're still there now, so they say, 40 or 50 of them, stranded and thrashing about on the beach."

# 11

# Waiting

A strange thing happened with those stranded whales. We got the full story a week later: it was headline news in *The Shetland Times*.

An oil slick had been spotted floating out from around the Terminal. An alert went out; and then the whales were seen.

They swam in from the Atlantic, heading south, slicing through the seething currents that separate the island of Yell from Mainland. The oil was drifting north towards them: they met it full on with the tide.

And when the whales came, the oil slick was halted.

It seemed to turn, said the coastguard, and others who had watched it. It seemed to turn and drift back to the place from where it came.

I asked my dad about it. He shook his head, white-faced. Oil was taboo, a forbidden subject now between us.

The whales followed the oil back, down Yell Sound, almost to the terminal. They swam in formation, skirting the islets: Muckle Holm, Little Holm, Little Roe and Lamba.

Then they seemed to turn and lose themselves: perhaps it was because of the tidal race, or the rocks and skerries, that they floundered, until at last they were thrashing blindly, washed up on the beach at the head of Orka Voe.

Naturalists went rushing there with ropes and

landrovers, to try and haul them back to safety. Many oil-men went to help, my dad among them, as if to try and purge their guilt.

But at this back-end of the year, nightfall came by mid-afternoon, the darkness thickened by sea-mist. It was impossible to do any more. The rescuers went home.

They came back at first light, but the whales were all gone.

It was claimed that they must have found their own way back to the water; but that couldn't explain the strange marks that were left behind.

For it seemed that small boats had been there, a whole fleet of them; and on the strand they'd left an odd tangle of ropes, plaited and knotted from leathery-brown seaweed.

Silently, secretly, who were the ones who had guided the whales back to the safe, far reaches of the sea?

Christmas came and went. A heavy, windless calm hung over the islands. It was ominous, the stillness of the frosty air, it felt as if the whole place was waiting.

And I seemed to be perpetually holding my breath. Dad was home over the holidays: we got on, in a way, but something like a cold abyss hung between us.

In January, the storms broke.

The winds were worse than anyone could remember.

They came from the north, straight off the sea, bringing sleet and the scent of the Arctic. They came from the west, sodden with rain, and east-born from the streams and mountains of Norway.

97

The waves thundered and spumed vicious, whipping froth over the rocks, and the great white birds screamed anguish from out of their winter silence.

In Lerwick, icy gusts blew down the steep lanes and across the shopping street, sending water high up over the old grey pier-heads. At home, the house shook, day and night, and along the way rocks broke off and went crashing from the cliffs.

In the wind, I sometimes fancied I could hear the Singing. And at night, I often dreamed about the whales.

I dreamed that I was weightless, deep in the wet, dark world of under-sea. The whales came to me; I could hear and feel their presence, and I was no longer afraid.

They sent thoughts into my mind's eye, like softly drifting shadows. They spoke to me, and in my dreams I understood.

I came to understand their sadness, their anger at the oil. Like a great black, spreading wound, it was to them. I understood why they sent messages and messengers to speak their anger and broadcast warnings.

*We have chosen you*, they seemed to tell me, *you must work to save us* . . .

And each morning I woke in a cold frenzy of tears: how could I explain to them my helplessness?

In the end, I spoke to Annie.

"Can you work something out for me on the computer? In whale-code?"

We were alone in the art-room together, stacking papers, tidying up pencils and brushes. She put down a clutch of things she'd been gathering, and turned to look at me.

"Tess—have you been hearing things again?"

"The Singing? No. But I've been dreaming about it."

"Now listen, Tess, I've been thinking. All this whale business—are you sure it's not just your imagination?"

"How ever can you say that, Annie? You met Miss Tait . . ."

"She's a loony. I'm just a bit, well, worried for you, Tess, that's all. You don't think you're going loony too? Hearing noises?"

"But Annie, what about Ranulf? You came to that club with me, and heard the things he said . . ."

"Another loony! Oh, and that reminds me of something else I've got to tell you. Jane's split up with Ran—well, that is, he's finished with her."

"When?"

"It was the night we followed them to the folk-club, the night the whales were stranded."

I sat down heavily.

"What happened?"

"Apparently he just wandered off and never came back to her. She hasn't seen or heard from him since."

"Is she upset?"

"She's pretty cut up." Annie tossed her hair back knowingly. "Mind you, I reckoned all along that he was just using her."

*Using her to get at me.* I shivered, and pushed the thought away.

"Anyway," I said, "*could* you work this out for me? A . . . a message of my own."

She shot me a pitying look, but the thing was, she

loved messing about with computers too much to resist that kind of request.

"Well, OK then. What do you want me to put into code?"

"Could you make something like, 'Please wait, I'm trying to help you'?"

"Don't be daft, Tess, we haven't got any key-words for anything vague like that."

I thought again.

"It's got to be simple," she said.

"How about, 'I come, go back, wait'?"

She closed her eyes and pondered for a few moments, mouthing something under her breath.

"I might be able to do something like that. I'll have a go. But Tess—"

"Well?"

"I still think you've gone over the top."

Nevertheless, before the week was out, she gave me the code of dots and dashes that I'd asked for; and when I was home on Saturday, I tramped carefully across the nearest stretch of cliffs with Freya in a howling snow-storm, hiding a large torch in my coat pocket.

I was too scared to walk far, or to stand close to the edge in that blizzard. I hoped no-one from home would see me.

And I hoped the whales might see my message.

I stood there, in a world of dull greys and swirling white: there was no other colour in the grass, the sky or the sea.

With the torch I flashed my message of long notes and short ones out into the emptiness.

No acknowledgement came. I waited for a few

moments until the cold and Freya's barking drew me homewards.

Next day the storms abated; but otherwise, nothing happened.

A deathly calm descended once more, the month rolled on and we all began to look forward impatiently to the explosion of fire and brightness that was Up-Helly-Aa.

# 12

# *Fire*

"Psst—Tess—up here!"

I looked round quickly in the damp, lamplit darkness.

Rob was standing at the far end of one of the lanes, waving madly. He called down to me, "The others have gone ahead. If we're quick, we'll get a good view at the burning site."

Sleet turned the paving stones smooth and gleaming. My feet clattered on the hard, uneven ground as I ran up to where he was waiting. The crowd milled thickly here, but Rob was small and nimble: he wormed a path through them and I followed.

We found Oliver and Annie right at the front of the gathering throng, near the playing fields.

Already we could hear the Up-Helly-Aa procession approaching, voices roaring out the traditional song. Over the brass-band, I caught snatches of the words:

> "*. . . wake the mighty memories . . .*
> *the ocean in its wrath . . .*"

Strong and drifting, they reached us through the revelry, but the night turned them bitter-sharp like icicles.

I stamped my feet, rubbed my hands, trying to get warm.

"Where's Jane?" I asked.

"Moping," said Oliver disdainfully.

"She hasn't got back with Ranulf then?"

Oliver shook his head. "I reckon he's disappeared off the face of the earth."

I wanted to discuss him more, but at that moment Rob exclaimed, "Hey, they're coming!"

We stood on tiptoe, and strained to see past people's shoulders. Light flared suddenly between the buildings.

The Jarl's Men were approaching, a squad of beefy fellows in full Viking dress, carrying their great dragon-headed longship high through a dazzle of flaming torches.

We could hear their singing clearly now, loud and gutsy, a roughcut stone of ancient celebration to melt the long winter's night.

At last they were upon us, turning into the field, torches lighting up grass and faces, bright as the sun. They formed round the towering ship: sleet and fire mingled; a bugle sounded. I blinked. When I opened my eyes again, a fireball lit the sky.

The men had flung in their torches to burn the ritual ship. Flames caught and the wood flared. Fire, fire, bright, warming! And then suddenly, the sky itself was ablaze!

For all above us now, light hung like a canopy of white-hot fire that swept across the heavens.

The whole crowd gasped: gaze was riveted upwards.

Here on the ground, the ship burned, but against the brilliant, flashing sky it was dim, feeble, insignificant.

Blinding, blinding, the sky was bearing down on us, a seething curtain of electricity. Reason told me it was only the northern lights, you often saw them on

sharp winter evenings like this; but terror was already within me, weeks of worry had stretched my reason taut. In the blazing sky I thought I saw patterns, and huge, drifting whale-shapes that wrote their anger into all that blinding whiteness.

And then a siren, sudden as a screaming arrow, pierced the night. Fire engines!

Tension snapped, people glanced round, new sounds filled the air and drowned the ritual songs.

The crowd was wild with excitement. The ship was burning, the sky was burning, something unforeseen had whipped the night alive. They began to shout, a rhythmic clapping, formless, tribal . . . and one after another, the fire engines went screeching past.

"What's going on?" I shouted, but no one heard. I poked Oliver in the ribs and asked it again. He looked down at me uncertainly for a couple of seconds, firelight dancing on the lenses of his glasses.

"Wait here—I'll try and find out."

He pushed a way out through the crowd. A few minutes later he was back: "Tess, there's something, um, something I'd better tell you. Can you come out."

My heart jumped.

"*What?*"

Oliver glanced round. "Bring the others."

We nudged Annie and Rob.

"We'll lose our places if we go," protested Annie.

Oliver was edgy and impatient: "It doesn't matter now."

He led us right outside the playing fields. Away from the crowd, the quietness of the street was unnerving.

105

I knew that whatever it was I had been dreading, would come now.

A group of men were standing just up the road, some of them in fancy dress. We could see them quite clearly in the unnatural light. They were talking with great agitation. I caught the words 'fire', 'terminal' and 'sabotage'.

More people appeared, running urgently back and forth across the street. A couple of blocks away, I heard car brakes screeching. The sirens had become an interminable wail.

"Tess," said Oliver, "this is it quickly. There's a fire on the terminal at Sullom Voe!"

Rob and Annie caught their breath. I felt numb; a slow sickness began to rise in me. I opened my mouth, but all I could get out was an idiotic "Wh-a-at?"

"A fire," Oliver became very calm and sensible. "Now listen. Is your dad working out there tonight?"

I could feel my lips trembling. I wanted to cry, but managed to hold it back.

"Yes. Yes. I think . . . I think he is."

"Are you sure?"

I tried to collect my thoughts.

"Yes Oliver, I'm sure."

"What started it?" asked Annie.

Oliver gestured at the men around us. "They don't know. There're just rumours. Must be an accident."

I said, "It's not an accident. I just heard someone say, it's sabotage."

"I told you," said Oliver quickly, "it's only rumours. People always invent things when there are no definite facts."

"Who made the fire?" I cried. The numbness was leaving me now, my nerves electric, I couldn't keep still. I grabbed Oliver by the shoulders and shook him. "Oliver, tell me, *who started the fire?*"

"Calm down Tess, I don't know. These things happen."

"They don't!" I screamed. "They've done it because I couldn't stop my dad! I couldn't save him!" Strangers' faced turned to look at me. "My dad's burning at Sullom Voe!" I yelled at them.

Someone tried to speak to me, but I didn't wait to listen. I started to run, blindly, down the street.

Oliver caught me up.

"Come on, Tess, we'll take you to our house."

"No! We've got to get to the Voe! I've got to save my dad!"

"He's probably all right," said Rob unconvincingly. "Perhaps he's not on the bit where the fire is."

"I told Annie I hated him. They gave me a chance and I couldn't get through to him. *I* made this happen!"

I heard them whispering behind, "She's gone hysterical."

Annie tried to put her arm round me and hug me like a baby. "Tess, don't be silly, of course it's not your fault."

I pushed her away. "It is, it is! They warned me!"

I found a tissue, blew my nose and went on, walking, then running again. "I don't hate him, I don't! It was just something I said because we'd argued." My eyes blurred. "I want my dad—I want him safe and alive!"

"Perhaps we ought to try and get her to her own home," said Oliver above my head.

"How?" said Annie. "There're no buses, and no hope of finding a taxi tonight."

"We'll have to hitch a lift then."

"That's dangerous," said Rob, "people get murdered and things."

"We'll be all right if we stick together."

Oliver caught me up and took my arm, calling to the others, "Come on!"

I was in a dream, or maybe it was a nightmare. My tears dried. We were running along a maze of streets towards the main road out of town.

Under the eerie sky-lights, it was a wilderness of garages, warehouses and docks.

I was aware of feeling cold and shaky. Oliver stood by the kerb and stuck out his thumb for a lift.

Cars whizzed past us. Their headlights seemed to rise and fall in an unkempt rhythm: there were long gaps between them and short ones. In the passing of the cars, I saw a pattern.

The whole world was full of patterns. Waiting there in the hopeless night, I was overwhelmed by them: we ourselves were mere dots, it seemed, in some great cosmic pattern: what happened to us now was beyond any control at all.

A car slowed and stopped. The driver leaned across to open the door. He was a middle-aged, featureless man: in the darkness his face was a mass of shadows, topped by an old tweed cap.

"Oh—kids." He hesitated. "Where you going then?"

"Place near Sullom," said Oliver.

"I'm heading north past there. But you looking for trouble, this time of night? Parents know you're out?"

"Please," said Annie, "don't ask any questions. Will you take us?"

"Cannot do no harm, I suppose. Hop in then."

Oliver sat in the front. Rob and Annie huddled, one on either side of me, in the back. The driver seemed drunk or nervy: it was a bumpy ride.

I stared straight ahead, between Oliver's shoulders and the driver's. The sleet had given way to rain: the windscreen wipers went phut-phut-phut; the headlights turned it into a sheet of steely silver.

We raced past villages, water and loneliness. The night sky became black again, and normal; the rain stopped. At last we came to the stretch of moorland that bordered onto Sullom Voe. From behind the curve of peat-bog, a new glow, the light from the terminal, set the sky ablaze.

"Oil's flaring bright tonight," remarked the driver.

"Could you drop us off now please," said Oliver quickly.

The car pulled up by the verge and we tumbled out.

"Hey—where you going to?"

Oliver gestured vaguely. "Turning we just passed. House down there. Thanks Mister."

The car roared off. Far away, we heard more sirens, and traffic turning down the road that led to the terminal; but in this place we were all alone.

"It is just up there, the turning to your house, Tess, isn't it?" said Oliver.

I nodded.

"Come on then, it's not that far to walk is it?"

I said, "Wait. I've got to see this fire. I've got to get to my dad."

I knew, from where we were, if you climbed a few hundred metres up over the moors, you could see the whole oil complex spread out in the distance below.

I struck out into the dead heather scrub. The ropey

stems stung and scratched round my ankles, my feet
sank into the sticky peat. The others caught me up,
muttering, trying to dissuade me: we trudged, four
abreast, in a slow heavy march to the top of the
hillock.

We stopped there and looked down.

# 13

## *Gone*

The terminal was lost in a sea of yellow flames.

Above it, the sky was ink-black. Where we stood, the hills were hard and still.

Cold seconds, minutes, maybe hours, went by.

At last Oliver said gently, "Tess, there's nothing you can do."

They were whispering behind me; I didn't care.

"Home," said Rob loudly. "Come on."

We found our way back to the main road. The firelight was behind us. There was nothing to say. We crossed over to the winding lane that led across the moorland to my house. It was four miles to the end. We walked without talking, on and on.

There was no moon or stars. The northern lights had long been quenched. And as we went, the oil blaze too slowly sank behind the hills like a sickly, misplaced sunset. I felt better when I couldn't see it any more.

Time lost all proportion. Shadows swallowed us up. We might have been trekking out there for eternity. Once or twice we stopped, crouching to rest while Annie caught her breath back, or Rob stuffed dead grass down his shoe to ease the pressure of a blister. I'd forgotten how to feel tired or scared. Numb, numb and empty . . .

As a white pencil-line of dawn cracked open the

sky to the east, we came to Miss Tait's house, quarter of a mile before my own.

I stopped before it, longing to see her. What did *she* know of the fire? What answers to a thousand mysteries lay hidden in her dusty rooms?

But Annie urged me onwards: "Don't stop now. We're nearly there."

None of us had spoken for an age. Words now sounded uncanny, hollow; my own voice came out dry and cracked.

"But Miss Tait—I want to ask her . . ."

"For goodness sake, Tess, forget about the old loony for now!"

"I can't. I can't forget her."

I stood there in the thinning twilight, vaguely remembering a lesson, something she had taught me, my head aching, puzzling at something that seemed wrong about the place, trying to bring back memories. Slowly something clicked.

"Oh—her boat's gone!"

I could just make out the bare patch in her garden where it had stood for all those years, immutable as a statue in the dead, tangled grass.

"Never mind that now!" Annie began to drag me after the others.

"Don't you *see*?" I said, "this *matters*." Unexpectedly, I found new reserves of energy and the thickness was clearing above my eyes. "It was always there, always! Covered in cobwebs . . . but now . . ."

I managed to hold Annie back. I called the others, almost as a scream: "Oliver, Rob, quick!"

The boys stopped, turned, raced back to us. Annie met them, there was an urgent flurry of whispers. They came to me: one side, the other side, the three

112

of them took my arms between them, to steer me gently away.

At the end of the road, I could see the chimney of my own house smoking.

I broke from them, back to the humped old cottage. I began to hammer with my fists upon the peeling door.

"Leave off Tess, idiot! She'll have fifty fits if you wake her!"

No answer: I banged again, over and over, until the skin was scraped from my knuckles. "Miss Tait!" I cried, "Jacobina! Let me in, oh let me in!"

The others caught me again: I pulled from them and fell heavily against the door.

It burst open under my weight, and I tumbled in over the treshold . . .

. . . into hollow, trickling silence.

The silence of an empty house.

I picked myself up and crept in: the others followed. Dawn washed through the open curtains. The furniture and bric-a-brac stood as it was. The hearth had been swept clean. A layer of new dust was gathering.

We gazed round the room. It was hushed like a museum.

"Jacobina?" I whispered; but only a small howl of wind outside made answer.

I went to the door which led to her back room and tried the handle: it gave at once. I opened it and looked in. It was completely bare.

I turned to the others: "The patterns have gone."

Rob said tremulously, "Let's get out. It's spooky. I've had enough."

We took one last look around the room.

"I think I'm dreaming," said Oliver.

113

"All of us?" said Annie. "In the same dream?"

"I feel so tired, anything's possible."

I closed my eyes for a moment, letting waves of anguish and exhaustion break over me until the tears were ready to come. *Burning, burning* . . . Oh, if only it were really no more than a dream!

"What's that?" cried Rob, and I jumped into wakefulness again. The others were standing, frozen, staring at the door.

"It's *her*!" breathed Annie. "There's someone outside!"

We waited, stretched to the utmost limits of endurance. Someone was rustling, poking through the grass and rubble round the step.

Then footsteps clomped in and a figure appeared.

I almost fainted.

My father was standing in the doorway.

# 14

## And Back to the Sea

His skin looked ashen-grey and there were deep
hollows under his eyes.

"What the . . . ?" He was staring as if we were
Martians.

"Dad," I said, "Oh *Dad*!" And then I fell sobbing
onto his large, familiar warmth.

"Good grief, what's this, what the devil is going
on?" He staggered slightly under me, then pushed me
gently away. "What's the matter and what the hell
are you all doing here?" His touch became rougher as
he realised the depth of our truancy. "How did you
get here, eh? All of you? Tess, I thought you were
staying with your friends in town tonight."

"Dad, oh Daddy, I thought you were dead!"

"Dead? What's got into you girl?"

"The fire . . ."

"Speak up girl. What fire? What's this all about?"

Oliver said, "The fire on the oil terminal, Mr
Jamieson."

"The *what*?"

"It ruined the whole festival," said Rob, "all those
fire engines whizzing around—we thought the whole
of Shetland was burned up!"

"But, oh Daddy, you're safe!"

"Of course I'm safe. But I still can't make head or
tail of this nonsense. Oliver, what's this you're saying
about a fire at the oil terminal?"

"Don't you know about it?" exclaimed Annie, "weren't you there?"

"No I wasn't! I left yesterday morning."

"But they must have rung you," I said. "They're *always* phoning you, for the least little bit of anything. You're always working yourself silly for them—surely you'd be the first to hear."

"Not any more," said Dad wearily. "I'm not working for them any more."

Oliver caught Annie's eye and nudged Rob. "If this is something private, Mr Jamieson . . ."

"It's open news as far as I'm concerned," said Dad. "I've quit."

"Oh," I said. "Oh Dad . . ." My knees felt all gooey; I looked around in a daze and found one of Miss Tait's rickety old chairs to sink into. The others stood fidgeting, looking embarrassed.

I said, "*Why?*"

Dad looked embarrassed too.

"I reached a point . . . there were things we could have stopped . . . totally unnecessary leaks—but the Board wouldn't have it. Money, money—it all comes down to the fact that they wouldn't chip a penny off their blasted profits. I argued with them, pleaded with them, even threatened them. In the end they gave me an ultimatum: to keep my mouth shut or get out.

"That was yesterday morning, Tess. I came home in the afternoon and discussed it over and over with your mother. We couldn't decide what I ought to do. It was the most difficult decision I've ever had to make in all my life. Everything we've built up here— to lose it—everything *you*'ve got here as well. And

116

then I remembered that, er, conversation we had, you and me, back before Christmas."

"Oh Dad, and I thought . . ."

"Yes, I know what you thought: that your old man didn't have the guts to make a stand." He paused and cleared his throat, almost nervously.

"Well, I've done it now, Tessa, I've done what you wanted me to do. I've put my conscience before my pay cheque. I've put saving the sea before saving us. I just hope to God I've done the right thing."

Through the windows, a pale sun was starting to rise.

"Well Tess?" He was waiting. "What have you got to say?"

"Oh Dad, you've done it! Thank you, thank you!" I threw myself at him, and this time he responded with the type of bear-hug he hadn't given since before the Singing started.

"Dad, I'm really proud!"

"Wait till the full consequences hit you," he muttered. "Wait until we have to pack up and go, because of what I've done . . ."

"I don't care, you've done what's right, that's all that matters!"

"Hmph. We'll have to see about that." He still sounded doubtful.

But Oliver said, "Congratulations Mr Jamieson. I'm *sure* you've done the right thing." He shook Dad's hand awkwardly.

"Absolutely," said Annie. "Good for you."

"Yeah!" said Rob, "Right on, Mr Jamieson!"

Dad flushed a little. "Right. Well. It's nice of you all to say so. Now. Where were we? What was I . . . ?" Oh yes. No, first we'd better get home and

117

find out about this fire. Oh—and I suppose you're all wondering what I'm doing here first thing in the morning? And for that matter, *you* still haven't told me what you're all doing here either. How did you get in? This is trespassing, you know, in Miss Tait's private house."

"We didn't mean to . . ." began Annie.

"It was Tess," said Rob.

Dad looked at me. "Well?"

"I wanted to see Miss Tait, that's all—I *had* to see her. Where is she, Dad? I was sure she'd be able to explain about this fire."

"The fire? Why her? This is beyond me."

"She knew about the Singing, you see, and the whales . . ."

"Tess, what *is* this?"

"You wouldn't understand," I whispered.

"But Mr Jamieson," interrupted Oliver quickly, "did you say you know what's happened to Miss Tait?"

"Ah," said Dad, "yes. In a manner of speaking. She's . . . gone. Left home—er, officially. But exactly when or where she's gone to . . . I was awake all night anyway, so I got up early and came along, to try and suss things out." He sounded as if he didn't quite believe it.

"Didn't she come and say goodbye to you then?" asked Rob.

"What's that? Goodbye? Her? No, not a word."

He pulled a sheet of crisp white paper out of his hip pocket and carefully unfolded it. "But this letter came yesterday morning. A solicitor's letter." He looked at me sharply. "There's something in it concerning *you*, Tessa."

118

"Me?" Things that had happened were jumbling in my mind. What would a solicitor want with me? Supposing I were in some way to blame for Miss Tait's going? Supposing I were guilty of some terrible crime to do with her?

The letter looked typed and formal, and ominously long.

"She's left something behind for you, it seems, that's all."

I must have looked really alarmed, because Dad grinned at me kindly. "Keep on guessing, Tess—it can wait until later. But come on, let's get home. Get some breakfast down us before there's any more talk."

He turned through the doorway and we followed him out, leaving deep, crude footprints in the dust. Then we squeezed into the car and bumped along the track to our house.

Dad took Mum aside as soon as we went in, and had words with her; then, tight-lipped, she cooked us eggs, bacon and toast for breakfast. As we ate it, Freya wrapped herself, panting, round and round my legs, then flopped down like a rug to warm my frozen feet.

Dad went into the hall to use the telephone. We heard him dialling over and over again, cursing. At last he got through, but we couldn't hear what he was saying.

He came back in.

"The fire's coming under control at last, but they're still fighting it. No-one's hurt. It started on the quay, in a building that was locked and empty; everyone got out in time."

"What's the damage?" asked Mum.

"Millions of pounds. It's a complete write-off."

119

"What does that mean?" I said.

"It means what I said." There was a curious note in his voice, as if he were smothering some private emotion. "A shut-down—the whole blasted new system—after all that! Finished. Completely destroyed. Thank God, is all I can say."

I hardly dared to ask it: "What about the oil leak?"

"That? Oh, there won't be any more of that! I told you, the whole pipe-line's cut off for now."

The other three went to ring their parents, to explain where they were. While they were out, I asked, "But how did the fire start?"

"They don't know," said Dad.

"Could it have been an accident?"

He shrugged. "There was nothing in the sheds where it started that could have caught light just like that. It's a mystery—a complete puzzle."

"Perhaps someone got in and started it?"

"There's tight security on that part of the complex. No one could get past that . . ."

"Unless," I murmured, "they came straight out of the sea."

He threw me a withering look, but there was affection in his eyes too.

"Ha ha."

I was too tired to consider it all any longer.

"Dad," I said, "tell me honestly—are you sorry you've left?"

"No," he said, staring at his shoes, "I'm not."

I began to pick my nails, working out what to say next.

"I . . . I'm sorry I thought bad things about you. It must have been ever so difficult to know what to do."

"All right, we all make mistakes. Just try and learn something from it, will you."

"I don't think you realise . . ." But of course, I couldn't even begin to explain myself. "Dad, are you glad we're talking to each other properly again?"

"What a daft question!" he said. "Yes, Tess, of course I'm glad."

Later on, he drove the Sinclairs home to Lerwick, planning to call on Miss Tait's solicitor while he was there. I was sent to bed; but, tired as I was, I couldn't get to sleep.

I got up again. "I'm going for a walk," I said to Mum.

She clucked around me, half protective, half still scolding for last night's adventure, but in the end she gave way, so long as I took Freya and didn't go far.

I never intended to break my promise; but when I got to the cliffs, Freya suddenly bounded away and refused to come when I called her to heel.

It was unlike her to disobey. She ran along the rabbit-bitten grass, waiting, barking, then on again before I could catch her up.

She squeezed under a wire fence: I followed over a stile. Beyond, the cliff dipped almost to the shore. She ran down, and wildly up the other side.

"Freya!" I called her, "Freya!" but that only sent her running faster, pausing anxiously now and then to see if I followed, then on again once more.

Our house was way out of sight. Mum would go spare if she knew where I'd got to. I stopped on top of the next ridge and looked around.

The day was white and still. The sea was calm. The far horizon was lost in a soft curtain of mist.

121

I could see Freya at the bottom of the next slope, looking back at me. She stood in a stony little valley, where a stream gurgled out between the cliffs and down a beach to the sea.

Then I started.

There was a man down there on the far side of the beach. A man and a boat.

Freya barked. The man looked up. He saw her, and then me. He stood watching, and in his distant gaze I felt a summons.

I climbed down the steep, grassy hillside grabbing at outcrops of rock to keep from falling, grazing my hands on broken shells.

The valley was sheltered and smelt strongly of seaweed. There was a line of stones you could step on to cross the stream.

I went over. Freya came to my heel now. The man waited, standing by his boat on the beach. I walked slowly towards him; the still little bay enclosed by soaring cliffs was like a lost world.

"Ranulf," I whispered.

He nodded, and his pale, sandy hair shook, reminding me of fronds of plants waving under water.

The blood was throbbing in my head, but I kept enough control to realise that this was my last chance.

"What's happening?" I said. "You've got to explain."

He shook his head.

"*Please* Ranulf, I feel so confused. Did *you* start the fire? I don't understand anything."

"Not now," he said. "I'm going home now."

I looked at his frail boat, then out to sea. The horizon was lost and empty.

He turned back to the boat, lifting it onto his

shoulders, and carried it across the pebbles to a white curve of sand. The waves lapped caressingly at his feet. He smiled down at them and placed his boat on the water. It bobbed up and down, up and down.

I went after him with Freya. She was cowering now.

"But will I ever see you again?" I asked. "Or Jacobina?"

He pointed with his toe at something stranded on the beach. It was a jellyfish, smooth and transparent. You could see right through its clear body to the sand that lay beneath. It was visible, yet *in*visible.

"We're like that," he said. "Mostly you'll look right through us; but sometimes you'll know that we're there. I hope you'll understand us some day, Tess— and some of the things that we did."

He waded right out into the sea, just as he was, pushing the boat before him. The water deepened as he went: when it was waist-high he turned back to me.

"So long then, Tess. Thanks for your help. And— remember us always, won't you?"

He hauled himself into the boat.

"Ranulf," I called, "Ran, come back! There's so much you haven't . . ." I thought of Dad's ashen face this morning. "Anyway, you were wrong about some things!"

"The danger's gone now, Tess, that's all that matters."

"And what about Jane? What can I tell her?"

He took up some oars and began to row straight out, strongly. With Freya at my feet I stood and watched him go, while a lump like grief began to rise in my throat. Out he went, growing smaller, more distant, a vague shape losing itself between ocean, horizon and sky. The mist hovered, waiting for him; then swallowed him up.

I called Freya and together we stumbled up the valley-side. From high up on the cliffs, I thought, we'd maybe get a better view. Perhaps we'd be able to spy him again, drifting out to sea.

At the top I strained, shielding my eyes against the glare. Once I thought I saw a black speck through the mist, that might almost have been a whale's fin; but it was too far away to be certain, and even as I stared, it seemed to disappear. And then I fancied I heard the echo of a song from off the waves, but when I tried to catch it, it faded again.

This time, I knew for sure, the Singing wasn't for me.

Dad came home, bearing strange news from the solicitor about Miss Tait.

"She's gone away—left the country apparently. But before she went, she made arrangements to tie up all her affairs and give away her possessions, like when someone dies and they make a will. This is what she left for you, Tess."

It was a brown paper package. I took it up to the solitude of my own room. Even before I opened it, I knew what I'd find inside.

It was the miniature oriental cabinet, with all the treasures still stored in its drawers and secret compartments; and right in the middle of its inner-most keep, was the tiny golden key.

Beside it, folded neatly, lay a note on soft blue paper, scrawled in a curiously elegant hand.

*To my dear friend Teresa*, it said, *because you alone heard the Singing and glimpsed some of the ancient secrets of the sea. Take care of your memories always. Here is the key to turn in whatever door you will. Yours affectionately, Jacobina Tait.*

I held the key in my hand for a few moments. It seemed very precious. Then I found a strong length of string, threaded it on securely and hung it round my neck.

Just as I had done so, the telephone rang.

Mum called: "It's Annie Sinclair for you!"

I belted downstairs.

"Hello Tess, have you got Miss Tait's present yet?"

I told her what it was; but she was impatient with her own news.

"Anyway, listen to this: I'm afraid we've lost the code for the Singing."

"Lost it?" I said.

"It got sort of jammed in the computer. The cassette that the program was on—it's broken—the whole thing! It's never happened before. I can't understand it. I'm ever so sorry, Tess."

"It doesn't matter," I said. "I don't think we'll be needing it any more. I somehow don't think I'll be hearing the Singing again . . ."

As I put the phone down, I felt a glorious sense of freedom, like a bird that's broken out from a cage.

It was some mystical pattern that *I'd* broken out of. I was free from all that strangeness. And round my neck hung the key to it all.